Will I pass as a good Puritan, Prudence?

Edward's eyes met hers with a query, and immediately she knew what he was asking. Would she help him to play the part—or denounce him as an impostor?

Normally she would have known no fear of the Oliverian militia—but being with Edward Hayward changed that completely. His danger suddenly became hers.

Olga Daniels was born in Norfolk and still lives there in a Broadland village. Her home is a picturesque flint and thatched farmhouse dating from the fifteenth century, which she and her husband renovated from a near-derelict condition. She has been writing for many years—articles, stories, books, and has also visualised for children's comics. She is fascinated by history, Scotland and romance. She has three sons and her interests include English folk dancing, rambling and gardening.

Previous titles

THE UNTAMED BRIDE
THE BRIDE FROM FARAWAY

THE
ARROGANT
CAVALIER

Olga Daniels

*First published in Great Britain 1991
by Mills & Boon Limited*

© Olga Daniels 1991

*Australian copyright 1991
Philippine copyright 1991
This edition 1991*

ISBN 0 263 77458 9

*Masquerade is a trademark published by
Mills & Boon Limited, Eton House,
18–24 Paradise Road, Richmond, Surrey, TW9 1SR.*

*Set in Times Roman 11 on 11½ pt.
04-9111-65464 C*

Made and printed in Great Britain

CHAPTER ONE

THE sun was warm that day in 1648. The man, dressed in a dishevelled buff-coat, lay in a thicket a short distance from the roadside. His sash of crimson marked him as an officer in the King's cavalry; his crumpled lace collar, the cut of his stained buff breaches and dusty bucket top-boots of finest leather showed him to be a man of wealth and fashion. It was late morning, and the sun was high in the sky, but he had only just awakened. Last night, well past midnight, he had staggered into the wood, crawled beneath a clump of young birch trees, dropped to a bed of pink-purple heather and almost immediately had fallen into a deep sleep of exhaustion.

Now the rumble of wheels made him stir to peer warily towards the track. He was well hidden, but as he lifted his head to see what was approaching there was an alert expression in his eyes and his muscles were tensed; his body ready to react swiftly to danger. Automatically his hand moved over to close on the loaded horse-pistol that he had placed, readily accessible, on the ling beside him.

A plodding brown horse came into his line of vision, pulling a small wagon covered by a hooped tilt. The driver appeared to be an elderly man— grey hair showed beneath his high-crowned black hat. The passenger was smaller, a woman wearing a bonnet-like linen cap that entirely concealed her hair and shaded her face. The man in the heather assumed that they were husband and wife and Puritans. They were dressed plainly, but they were not poor country folk, for their black clothes were obviously expensive. The wheels crunched on the rough stones of the road—the cart was heavily laden.

As the cart drew alongside that place where he crouched the woman moved her head, and he glimpsed the smooth skin of youth, a wisp of fair hair, keen eyes that seemed to be trying to penetrate the thicket which concealed him. He noticed the prim set of her lips, though they were sweetly shaped; a typical Puritan maid, he thought with little pleasure. He allowed himself to relax. They had not seen him and therefore posed no threat to him. He gave a wry smile; he must be weary indeed not to feel the least response to the sight of a comely wench! He allowed his mind to play briefly with the question as to whether she was really as prudish as her expression had suggested, then dismissed the thought. He had no interest in the couple other than to wonder vaguely where they might be going on this road through the wood that was so little used. The cart rolled on, and as the crunch of its iron-shod wheels began to fade he relaxed. Lying back, he stretched long, lean limbs and flexed powerful muscles; in spite of everything, he was glad to be alive—and intended to remain that way if possible.

It was only a few days since the armies of Cromwell had beaten the Royalist forces at Preston, and, here in East Anglia, Colchester had been forced to surrender to Fairfax after a siege of more than two months. Dark days they were, with families split in their loyalties, never knowing whom to trust.

The same terrible strife of Civil War that had caused the Cavalier to sleep rough among the bracken and heather had also been instrumental in persuading Jacob Collins to set off with his daughter, Prudence, on this hazardous journey. They were on the first stage of it, with thousands of miles ahead which would take them from their native city of Norwich, away to a different land, a new world.

'Pray God we shall be in time to board the ship before she sets sail,' muttered Jacob.

'Amen to that, Father.'

Though not normally of a nervous disposition, Prudence shivered and drew her cloak closer around her shoulders. There was something sinister in the impenetrable darkness below the trees. Surely the road to the port should be wider than this? Why did they meet no other travellers? During the previous two days they had been on the journey they had never encountered a track so deserted and rough.

'Are you sure we're on the right road, Father?' she asked.

'How can I be sure of anything?' he shrugged. 'This part of the country is unfamiliar to me, but you heard what the innkeeper said. He assured me it was a short cut.'

Prudence was about to remind her father that she had tried to dissuade him from acting on that advice, but she closed her mouth. There was no point now in repeating it. He had trusted the man, partly perhaps because of the need for speed—because of his fear that the boat would sail without them. She had not dared to mention the way the landlord's leering eyes had devoured her when Jacob had been saying grace before their evening meal—because her own eyes should have been demurely downcast, if not tightly closed. It had been her mistrust of the man that had made her look up when she should have been concentrating on the holy words, but that was no excuse.

Even had she mentioned it her father might have accused her of imagining it, as he had done when she had spoken of a similar expression on the face of one of the elders of the church. 'Vanity is a sin,' Jacob had warned her sternly. 'Because you are young and comely you must take especial care not to flaunt yourself before men.'

'I don't flaunt myself, Father,' she had pleaded. 'It just happens.'

'Vanity. That's all it is—vanity,' he had repeated, and closed the subject.

When they had left the Cross Keys that morning she had pleaded with her father to keep to the main road as he had originally intended, but he had been adamant. She remembered uneasily that the innkeeper had been unduly inquisitive about the purpose of their journey too. The cart rumbled on, jolting into and out of deep ruts dried by the summer sun from the mud that would cover the way in winter. Apart from the sound of the wheels there was an uncanny silence; no wind stirred, no bird sang. Prudence sat rigidly upright, her unease increasing as the trees seemed to close over in front of them, shadows deepening, darkly sinister—was there a movement in those bushes?

She stared harder. There it was again—on her side of the track and no more than two yards ahead, a shaking of leafy twigs when there was no wind. Something—or someone—was there! She glimpsed the pale colour of flesh—a hand—and in it, its barrel catching a shaft of sun, a pistol.

'Father——'

The word became a scream as two wild-looking men sprang out. One held a pistol and was pointing it directly at them. The other, brandishing a long cudgel, ran towards the head of the horse. Both men were roughly dressed with fierce bearded faces, unkempt, outlaws bent on plunder—or worse.

'Stop the cart, old man,' growled the man with the pistol.

Jacob slapped the horse's rump with the reins, stirring it to move faster. He took hold of the whip, an instrument he was not in the habit of using.

'Stop—or I shoot!'

'Giddup,' Jacob urged.

The horse quickened its pace. Jacob swung the whip, not towards the animal, but at the ruffian with the pistol. A shot rang out.

'Father!' screamed Prudence.

He turned pained eyes towards her. Horror gripped her in breath-stoppping agony as she saw blood spurt from his chest. He would have fallen from the cart, but she threw her arms around him. A great shuddering racked his body so strongly that she felt it herself, physically, and she had not the strength to hold him. Despite her frantic efforts, he slumped forward to the rocking floor of the cart. The horse reared up and would have bolted, but the other man grabbed its bridle, jerking it viciously to bring the animal down and force it to stand still.

'Father—oh, my dear, dear Father——' His shuddering stopped and he lay still, his eyes staring, mouth open; in numb disbelief Prudence knew there was nothing she could do for him. A hand clutched at her arm. Terrified, she turned, and saw a dirty, lewd face with a broken-toothed grin.

'Well—this is a dainty morsel, just as that owd devil of a landlord said. Get down here, wench, and let's have a proper look at you.'

She tried to draw back from him but he was far too strong. His grip tightened. Roughly he tried to pull her from the cart, his hand twisting in the fine woollen cloth of her black dress. Helplessly she felt herself slipping towards him. She struggled to keep her balance, desperate to avoid the clutching hands reaching for her. Self-preservation told her she must land on her feet. If she fell he would be on top of her in a moment and she would have no chance to get away. By sheer determination she managed to keep her balance when her feet struck the ground and she immediately tried to dodge to one side. She was sickened by the smell of his noxious breath as he reached out a hand and grasped the neck of her bodice and pulled her closer to him.

'Murderer!' She spat the word at him. 'Let me go!'

She pulled and twisted, but he held on to her. Her bodice ripped and she could feel the roughness of his fingers against her bare flesh, just above her breasts.

'There's no one to hear you, my pretty.' He laughed at her violent struggles, braggingly sure of himself, uncaring and unhurried.

Terror gave her extra strength. She tugged against his hand, which twisted more tightly into her bodice, then in desperation she lowered her head and bit hard into the disgusting flesh of his filthy fingers. As her strong, healthy teeth sank in she tasted the blood that spurted sickeningly into her mouth and knew she had hurt him. He yelped like a kicked cur and released his hold.

It gave her a chance. She twisted her supple young body, saw his arm shoot out to strike her, and ducked under it. Her cap was knocked from her head, and she grabbed hold of her long, cumbersome skirts and ran. She made for the woods, though she knew she had only a brief advantage. It was sheer panic that drove her on. The ruffian gave a terrifying snarl and his heavy footsteps thudded, snapping twigs as he set off in pursuit.

'You bitch! I'll teach you a lesson you won't forget!'

She dared not glance back. She ran on, but even when she reached the trees—how would she manage to dodge through them? She tugged frantically at her skirt, which had caught on a bramble.

'You won't get away...' He seemed to be closer '...Puritan whore—when I catch you——'

His words changed to a scream as a shot rang out. Prudence glanced back and saw the robber stagger to his knees. He remained there for a few seconds, almost as if in supplication, then he pitched over and lay prostrate on the ground. Back along the track, a man was running towards her. The scarlet sash and the cut and quality of his clothes told her he was a King's man, even though everything he wore was rumpled and unkempt. He held a smoking pistol in his hand. She stood still, too shocked and terrified to do anything other than remain where she was. She had been saved from that ruffian—but what now? Could she trust a Cavalier? Should she keep running?

'Stay where you are,' he called out to her.

'Dear God—help me,' she prayed fervently. She could do nothing but obey his command because it suddenly seemed as if all strength had drained from her. Instinctively she caught at the wickedly torn material of her bodice, drawing the ragged blood-stained remnants together as closely as she was able in a futile attempt to cover her shoulder and breast with a semblance of modesty.

The stranger did not approach her but moved quickly towards the cart. The second ruffian was there—he had been riffling beneath the covers when the shot disturbed him. Now he jumped down, and as the Cavalier raised his pistol, aiming it in his direction, the man dodged away, using the horse and cart as cover, and hared for the wood. Within seconds he was out of sight among the trees and undergrowth. The Cavalier ran on, as if intending to give pursuit, then stopped, still alert, staring into

the trees. A few seconds later even the crashing
sound of the ruffian's feet and the snapping of twigs
died away. Prudence shuddered, relieved to see him
go. She caught the eye of the Cavalier.

'T'would be futile to follow him,' he said.

'Yes,' she agreed. Her voice was little more than
a whisper. With an effort she made herself recover
something of her self-control. Bewildered, scarcely
knowing what she was doing, she began to walk
slowly towards the cart.

'Stay where you are,' commanded the Cavalier.

She turned numbed eyes towards him. 'I must
see to my father.'

'I fear there is nothing you can do.'

'I must see to him,' she repeated. She knew that
he was dead—he had fallen in her arms, with blood
gushing from his heart—and yet a part of her refused to accept the fact. It could not really be true.
Not her beloved father. He was her only living rela-
tive apart from an uncle she had never seen, away
in far-off New England. She walked on, but before
she reached the cart the stranger stepped in front
of her. Gently but firmly he grasped her upper arms
and moved her aside.

'Stay there, mistress. I will see to your father.'

She opened her mouth to protest, but, numbed
by shock, she could only stand as he'd directed. He
strode to the cart, where the body of Jacob Collins
was huddled in a pool of blood. She watched in
misery as he leaned over and closed the staring eyes,
then he climbed up and dragged the body from the
driver's seat until it was lying inside the wagon. He
pulled a tilt over to cover it, then, standing up on

the footboard, looked anxiously all around.
Prudence read the need for caution in his face—
the robbers might have accomplices. She held her
breath, but there was no sound from the woods
except for the soughing of a light breeze in the
branches and the cooing of a pair of pigeons some
way off.

The Cavalier leapt down and moved over to the
ruffian he had shot. He rolled the inert body over
with his foot, then bent down and closed those eyes
also. She watched in numbed disbelief as he pro-
ceeded to remove the dead man's coarse leather
jerkin, stripping off his own torn buff-coat and lace-
trimmed collar, then, after fastidiously shaking the
other man's garments at arm's length, shrugged
himself into them. He did not change his shirt, but
tore the lace from the cuffs of it and knotted a red-
spotted kerchief around his neck. His appearance
was quite changed—he no longer looked the
Royalist officer she knew him to be.

He bundled up his discarded clothing, looked
around for a moment, then walked to the edge of
the wood and stuffed it all deep into a hollow tree.
Coolly he picked up the pistol with which her father
had been shot, and placed it in the cart, then walked
over to Prudence.

She had watched his every movement with a
strange sense of unreality, knowing him to be an
enemy, conscious of her own helplessness, her brain
half numbed by the horror of the last few minutes.
Her dear father was dead—and she dared not think
what would have happened to her but for the timely
arrival of this tall, hard-faced Cavalier, this stranger

with the commanding presence. Who was he? What was he doing on foot in this lonely place? Could she trust him? She had heard horrific stories of the callousness, cruelty and lust of the officers and men of the Royalist army. He came towards her and instinctively she drew back, yet made a determined effort not to show her fear, thrusting her head up to face him bravely. She clutched at the ragged bodice of her gown, which had been entirely ripped off one shoulder; the stomacher which should have covered the lacings was lost. Despite her efforts, the torn material refused to close, revealing the delicate curve of bare flesh at the top of her breast.

'Get back on the cart, mistress,' he said.

She took one step forward, but shock seemed to have weakened her and her knees wobbled alarmingly; she needed to hold on to something for support, yet dared not take her hands away from her torn gown. The trees began to float nauseatingly around and she would have slid to the ground, but the man caught her. His hands gripped her upper arms, as if he would have shaken sense into her. The strength of his grip helped her to fight against that feeling of faintness.

'Pull yourself together!' His voice was authoritative. 'We must get away from here.'

Prudence took a deep breath and steadied herself. She must keep her wits about her. She was a grown woman; childhood had ended early for her when her mother had died. After that she had taken over the running of the household for her father, and had helped him in his business also. Her mouth set in a firm line of determination. Now she was alone, but somehow she had to cope. She felt the hands of the stranger digging into the soft flesh of her arm where her sleeve was torn. It reminded her she must do something about her disgraceful appearance. She wrenched herself from his hold and he let her go. She walked unsteadily, but with iron-willed determination, to the back of the cart.

Before she had even lifted a corner of the tilt he was there beside her. 'What are you doing now?' he asked in a tone of exasperation.

'I must change——'

'This is no time for foolish vanity—that ruffian who escaped may come back at any moment, and when he does he won't be alone. We must get away from here.'

Part of her knew what he said was right, but another instinct said she had to get out of her ripped and soiled dress. 'It's not vanity——' she began.

He swung her up into his arms.

'Let me go...' she cried.

He ignored her words. She pummelled at his hard chest with her hands. It had no effect upon him. He strode around the cart and threw her up unceremoniously into the seat where but fifteen minutes earlier she had been riding beside her father. She sat still, in shocked silence. How could she travel on looking like some disreputable wanton? Had the stranger not noticed the state her dress was in? She opened her mouth to protest, but the Cavalier was already striding forward, and his broad-shouldered, straight back was intimidating. Fuming but helpless, she knew he would take no notice of anything she said to him, and her lips set in a taut, thin line. Then she glanced around and fear again gripped her in the pit of her stomach: danger still lurked in the impenetrable darkness of the wood; anything—anyone—might be there, hidden beneath the overhanging trees. She shuddered.

The horse had lowered his head to graze contentedly on a patch of lush grass. It resented being disturbed when the man took hold of the bridle, and tossed its head, but only momentarily. It knew the hand of a master and obeyed. The cart rocked as the man led the animal back on to the track, then, unlooping the reins, he hoisted himself with one fluid movement up into the driver's seat.

'Which way?' he asked, turning towards her. 'Onward or back?'

'Onward,' she said immediately. 'I have nothing to go back for.'

'I'll take you home,' he said, not understanding her.

'That you cannot do, sir, for I have no home.' The feeling of being bereft deepened.

'How so?' Surprise showed plainly in his face.

'All the home we—I have is on the wagon.'

He glanced behind him, taking in the sparsity of goods beneath the tilt, as if digesting that information. 'You don't look like a gypsy.'

'Indeed I am not! My—my——' she paused and drew in a deep gulping breath before she could continue '—my father and I were on our way to the port of Harwich, where we were to board a vessel bound for New England.'

'You mean—you are about to leave the country?' One expressive eyebrow twitched upwards in surprise. 'You intend to join that mad bunch of ranters out in America among the heathen?' He seemed to find the idea so bizarre that he laughed out loud.

'Yes,' she replied sharply, and snapped her lips together tightly, angered by his response. She looked straight in front of her, with her head held high.

There was a brief moment of silence between them, then he nodded. 'Onward, you said. Then so be it. One thing is sure: we must not sit here discussing the matter.'

He slapped the reins on to the horse's rump and set the animal going at a smart pace. The rumble of the wheels and the clip of the horse's hooves when they struck a stone was somehow soothing in its ordinariness. They travelled on, and the Cavalier was silent for several minutes, though he glanced around and back over his shoulder many times.

'If you were on your way to Harwich why the devil were you travelling on this road?' he asked suddenly, as if speaking a thought aloud.

'It was the innkeeper at the Cross Keys, where we stayed last night, who directed my father this way.'

'That nest of evil! The scoundrel! He must have been in league with those outlaws.'

'He said it was a short cut,' she said bitterly. 'Unfortunately my father believed him.' She closed her eyes—if only he had not taken that evil advice!

'This road leads only to the village of Thickby.'

'But will it take us to Harwich?'

'Eventually.' His tone was dry.

She scanned his face anxiously, seeking some re-assurance. 'We were supposed to be travelling to Harwich by way of Tillington, where we hoped to meet up with others from our area who are bound for America.'

'We can get to Tillington on this route, that is sure——'

'Perhaps we should turn round——'

'And risk going through those woods again? No. You made the correct decision when you said "onward". Let us abide by it. Giddup!'

The Cavalier slapped the reins briskly on to the horse's rump, getting much more pace out of the animal than Jacob had ever managed to, so that the goods in the back of the wagon jolted alarmingly. She glanced covertly at this man beside her, trying to assess some of his character from his appearance.

She judged him to be about thirty years of age, and he was very tall and broad-shouldered. He was bare-headed and his hair had been roughly cut to just below his ears. Its ends were so ragged that she formed the opinion that it had been hacked at with a pair of sheep-shears, yet she had to admit that it was attractive, waving in tawny disarray around his strong face.

His head was held up proudly—she was not surprised by that, for she had heard that gentlemen of the King's army were arrogant, though she had never before been in such close company with one. He had taken it for granted that he should accompany her, and had taken over the reins of her cart as if he were the owner, giving her no option. He looked cool and calm—as a soldier, no doubt, he had witnessed death many times, and this was not the first time he had killed. To him the tragedy and drama of the last few minutes were probably commonplace. Even now, with the scene of the attack well behind them, he remained alert, poised to deal with any more trouble that might come, his eyes darting from one side of the narrow track to the other.

His face was not an easy one to read. Something in his bearing told her that life's conflicts had touched him closely, hardened him—yet he had been gallant in springing to her rescue. For that she had to be grateful. She had heard that Colchester had fallen to the Roundheads—had this man been among those routed in the battle? If he was on the run perhaps somehow she could use that to her advantage. She reminded herself that she had one very powerful asset—if she could keep it safe.

Beneath her seat was a strong wooden box, bound with iron bands and padlocked. It contained papers and permits for the voyage, and a few items of jewellery which had belonged to her mother and were now hers. There was also a bag of gold coins. She reached down surreptitiously with one hand, simply to reassure herself that it was indeed safely there. The key—— She drew in a sharp breath, remembering that the key was tucked into the money-belt strapped around her father's waist. She must make sure that no one saw it, that the belt was handed to her intact.

Though she was by nature open and trusting, she knew that now she must be careful. No one—not this man beside her, nor any other person—must find out about contents of the box. Assuredly the time would come when she would need that money to buy assistance. A strong instinct for survival asserted itself, taking over her brain; she must move cautiously. And as a start she must try and find out something about this handsome, domineering stranger.

'I think it is time we introduced ourselves,' she said tentatively. 'I am Mistress Prudence Collins. Pray, sir—what is your name?'

He did not answer immediately, but appeared to concentrate with undue attention as the horse negotiated a particularly deep rut in the track. Then he looked at her with a disarming directness that she found strangely disconcerting. When at last he spoke his voice was pleasantly even, with a resonant, slightly throaty timbre. It set up a tingly alertness in her.

'Mistress Prudence Collins.' He repeated her name, rolling it over on his tongue as if deliberately weighing up its merits. Ridiculously she hoped he would like it, but there was a sarcastic twist to his lips as he said, 'Aye, that sounds about right.'

He sounded dismissive, and absurdly she was hurt. It emphasised their differences, as if she did not know already that there could be only enmity between them—he a Cavalier and she a Puritan. After a pause he said, 'I am called Edward Hayward.'

His hesitation made her doubt whether he spoke the truth, even though he had turned his head in her direction and his eyes held hers with apparent honesty. She thought it more than likely that he had cause to hide his identity, but decided that dissimulation was a game that two could play at. She would pretend to believe him.

'I have to thank you for coming to my rescue, Master Hayward,' she said. She intended to keep her voice brisk, but that was easier said than done as a shudder trembled over her. She gripped her hands tightly together to steady herself. She could easily be overwhelmed with emotion if she allowed her mind to dwell on those dreadful events.

'It was my privilege to be of service,' he replied laconically.

He spoke as if it was nothing, but on this point the truth, for her, was absolute. 'You put yourself in danger for my sake, sir. I shall never forget that.' She lowered her voice and added with breathless sincerity, 'How fortunate it was that you happened to be there at that precise moment.'

'Perhaps that is something you should forget.'

'I couldn't——' she began, and then broke off.

She would never forget how he had looked in that moment when she had first seen him running up the lane towards her, holding a smoking pistol in his hand, his buff-coat crossed with the crimson sash, lace at his throat and cuffs. He was an officer in the King's army, one of the oppressors, an enemy of the plain people—perhaps, like her dear dead brother, he had fought at Naseby. She shuddered. He might even have fired the shot that had killed

Ralph. No, she would never forget how this man had looked, that he was on the wrong side of this dreadful conflict—and nor would she ever forget the horror of the certain fate from which he had saved her.

She shook her head and murmured softly, 'I take it you are referring to your appearance, sir?'

A slight smile lifted muscles in his lined face, brought life to his eyes, which, she suddenly noticed, were of a warm hazel colour. 'Exactly.'

'Have no fear on that score.' Instinctively she smiled back at him, wanting to show that he could trust her. 'Should anyone ask I assure you I shall remember you dressed exactly as you are now.'

His eyes flickered speculatively over her face. He liked her steadfast, honest expression, could not help but see the beauty in her delicate, regular features. It occurred to him that those large eyes, which were quite startlingly blue, would have captivated half the gallants at court had she been one of the fine ladies there. He had no patience with Puritans and their cold repressive ways, but most certainly it would be a challenge to awaken an amorous response in this comely wench. He allowed his eyes to rest on the soft roundness of her deliciously pink lips—undoubtedly very kissable. He pulled himself up sharply. Despite her promise, he could not be sure of her. He must not forget that they were on opposite sides in this conflict—made worse for him now that there seemed to be little hope that the King would be victorious.

Prudence was aware of his scrutiny and drew her tattered garments around her. What lay ahead of her? Was he an honourable man? She was acutely aware that he had a man's strength—just as those ruffians had—and she had nothing but her wits to protect her. Her fervent hope was that they would prove nimble enough to suffice.

CHAPTER TWO

EDWARD allowed the horse to proceed at a leisurely pace. He turned towards Prudence. 'I take it you intend to carry on with this plan to leave the country?' He sounded disapproving.

'What else can I do? I have no home here.' Even if she had, she would not wish to go back. Truly she had nothing to return to.

'Tell me more about your family, Mistress Collins. You said there was only your father and you?'

'Once there were four of us; now there is only me.' Her heart was heavy as she thought of it. 'My brother was killed at Naseby. My mother died of the pestilence many years ago. You know what has happened to my father.'

'These are terrible times we live in,' he said.

'Terrible, indeed,' she agreed.

There was silence between them for a short time. Then, prompting her again, 'You mentioned that you came from Norwich?'

There could be no harm in answering such straightforward questions, and suddenly it was a relief to talk. 'I was born there, and have lived there all my life. I've kept house for my father since my mother died, though I was but twelve years of age at that time. More recently I have also helped my father with his business.'

'And your father was...?'

'Jacob Collins, a woollen merchant, dealing mainly in Worstead cloths.'

'You have no other relatives?'

'There is only my uncle, my father's brother, though I have never seen him. He went to New England some twenty years since, when I was but a babe in arms. He has written several times suggesting that we should join him out there. I believe he now has a fine house and land—a farm which is profitable. My father was loath to leave our home in Norwich. He had a good business, and we had much in life to be grateful for, until these troublesome times. Not that my father took any part in politics. He was too old to ride off to battle and too wise not to see that there was good and bad in both sides. But the effects of it came to us despite this.' She paused.

'Tell me about it,' he said, and his voice was surprisingly gentle.

'Well, things came to a head last month when there was rioting in the street. I have no idea which side started it or what it was all about, but there was a great disturbance in the city, and then two groups of men were fighting in the square just outside our house. They were carrying sticks and cudgels and flares, and in the course of it our house was set on fire. My father's warehouse was part of the premises and all the merchandise was burned— dozens of bales of finest woollen material and the house itself and a greater part of its contents all went up in flames.' She shook her head, remembering how awful it had been—and yet it was as nothing compared to today's tragedy.

'I'm sorry to hear of it,' Edward Hayward said.

'All those years of work and effort destroyed in an hour or so! The few pieces on the wagon behind us are all that were left. My father was a broken man; he had no heart to build up his business all over again. I persuaded him that he should accept my Uncle Benjamin's invitation and join him in this new world.'

'You persuaded him?' Edward Hayward sounded surprised.

'Most certainly. You may think it an unusual decision for a woman to take, but my father had come to trust my judgement in many matters. There was nothing here to hold me.'

'You were not affianced to any man?'

'No. I have been needed to keep house for my father. It would have been different but for this dreadful civil war. Had my brother not been killed.' Although she knew it was provocative, she could not resist adding, 'They were fighting to uphold the rights of men.'

'Many young men have been slain, on both sides,' Master Hayward said simply. Then he added sadly, 'Far too many.'

A moment later he was questioning her again. 'But you? Did you not wish for marriage, for a home of your own?'

'I do not know many young men, Master Hayward.' She paused, then added, 'I have been— content.'

She wished she had been able to say that with more conviction, for he was looking at her with those intelligent eyes of his, and his eyebrows quirked upwards as if he did not quite believe her. An amused smile played on the corners of his lips. He made her embarrassingly aware of how inexperienced she was—if not entirely in the ways of the world, at least in the art of coquetry. She felt almost as if he guessed at that wicked yearning that had sometimes made her feel rebellious about the staidness of her life, that restlessness which had driven her to persuade her father to set out on this long journey to the New World. Perhaps she was being punished for it. She clenched her small hands into tight fists and fought back the tears that threatened to flood her eyes. She fumbled for her kerchief, wiped them away and braced herself to look squarely at the future. She reminded herself that she had considerable expertise in the Worstead business, and was well capable of organising her own life.

'When I reach New England my uncle will give me a home,' she said. 'And he has said that he will easily arrange a suitable marriage for me.'

'I have no doubt of it!' The sarcasm of his tone angered her.

There was a short silence, broken only by the rhythmic clip-clop of the horse's hooves, the jingle of harness, the crunch of wheels. Then he said, 'It's a long journey to make to find a husband.'

'Sir! You misunderstand me,' she snapped. 'I have to look at the future seriously; I am not a silly maiden whose head is full of notions of romance.

I know that in the New World women have to work hard beside their men in order to tame the wilderness, but I am prepared for that, and because of it I expect marriage to be a true partnership.'

'What a truly practical little Puritan you are, Mistress Collins.'

'I am as I am,' she remarked, pursing her lips in a prim line. 'But you—you have told me nothing of yourself. Are you making your way home—to a wife and family, perhaps?'

'Like you, I have no home or family. My past is not important. All that matters to me now is that I exist.'

He trusted her even less than she did him—that was obvious! The misery of her situation threatened to overwhelm her. She would have given everything—every ounce of gold that was in the little box under the seat of the wagon—if only she had not persuaded her father to leave Norwich! But, agonising though it was, nothing she could do now would ever alter that. She must go on. Her father would have expected her to. That thought helped her to regain a measure of her customary quiet, resolute self-control. She turned to the man who sat beside her and wondered again—as she had done interminably since she had seen him running towards her with the smoking pistol in his hand, dressed as an enemy, a gentleman of the King's army—would he turn out to be a friend or a foe?

She had to find out more about him, for how else could she assess whether it would be safe for her to remain in his company—or whether to escape as soon as opportunity arose? 'May I ask in which direction you intend to travel, Master Hayward?'

An ironic smile lifted one corner of his shapely mouth, as if her question amused him. 'Wherever chance takes me,' he said. 'Like you, I have nothing to turn back for.'

She thought anxiously of the gold she had in the box beneath her seat and wondered what he would say—or do—if he discovered it. People had been killed for less. 'This place we are heading for—what did you call it?'

'Thickby.'

'Shall we reach it before nightfall, Master Hayward?'

'If all goes well.'

She took comfort from that and sat still and quiet, deliberating, keeping her eyes fixed on the road ahead.

A mile further along, the road emerged from the cover of the wood and snaked across a flat plain. It was the usual, familiar open field culture, golden with ripening corn. The wide field was bathed in a dry glow of sunshine, the horse slackened its pace and she noticed that Master Hayward relaxed a little. No longer was he staring vigilantly around, alert for hidden dangers in the wood, and unnervingly she found him gazing at her with shrewd perception. His eyes were so dark as to be almost black—and in the unfathomable depths of them there was a disconcertingly bold arrogance. Something in that look, and the touch of excitement it roused in her, flashed a warning. It made her feel even more vulnerable than she had before.

She lifted her chin to return his look of appraisal with a defiance that was rather touching had she but known it. She was uncomfortably aware of the manner in which those bold eyes raked her, and she clutched nervously at the torn fabric of her bodice. The sleeve had been ripped from the shoulder and across almost to the neckline, and the rest of the garment was torn so irrevocably that a most immodest amount of white rounded flesh was visible. Colour blazed into her face.

'I pray you, stop the cart, Master Hayward,' she commanded. 'Over there by that old hut.' He raised one quizzical eyebrow, and she said quickly, 'I must change my gown and make myself more presentable.'

He ran a discerning eye over her and a smile quirked at one corner of his shapely mouth. 'Aye. You would certainly attract an uncommon rush of curiosity if you drove into Thickby looking so.'

He drew the horse to a halt beside the simple timber hut which served as a shelter for the shepherd at lambing time. It was empty at this time of the year. Edward leapt down and came round to her side of the cart, holding up his arms to assist her down. The simple manoeuvre was rendered exceedingly difficult by her embarrassed attempt to hold together her torn bodice and lift her skirts so that they should not catch beneath her feet. Indeed, even as she contemplated the best way to accomplish her descent, the horse took a step forward and she overbalanced.

She felt herself falling. Then the instinct for self-preservation overcame modesty. She released her

hold on her gown, reached out with both hands to
save herself and was precipitated into his open arms.
At once they clamped tightly around her, holding
her close and safe, and when she looked up at him
breathlessly his eyes smiled down into hers with a
positively devilish air.

She pushed her hands against the hard wall of
his chest. He released her immediately, and her
hands flew back to gather together the shreds of
her bodice. She was horrified to find that the
material had ripped even further, deeper towards
her waist. His eyes dropped from her face to the
roundness of her breast. No man had seen her so
near-naked before. She crossed her arms closely to
cover herself and spoke imperiously.

'Turn your back at once, Master Hayward.'

That disconcerting smile still played with the
corners of his mouth and twinkled in the near-
blackness of his bold eyes. For a brief moment she
thought he would ignore her request, then in a
leisurely way he shrugged his shoulders, signifying
indifference, and moved towards the head of the
horse.

Prudence hurried round to the back of the
wagon, lifted the tilt and looked inside for the
bundle that contained her clothes. She was thankful
that it was tucked at one side and within easy reach,
so she did not have to disturb the dark heap that
was the lifeless body of her father. She closed her
eyes and whispered a prayer for the soul of that
man who had been so dear to her, yet she dared
not linger there too long for fear that Edward
Hayward might become impatient. Taking the

clothes into the shelter of the hut, she changed as quickly as possible, then thrust her discarded gown into the wagon, hoping that she might be able to repair the damage, extensive though it was. Feeling much more in command of herself, she walked round to rejoin her companion.

Edward Hayward lounged on the grass at the side of the track. He uncurled his long, lean frame, stood up as she approached and ran a discerning eye over her. No one could fault the modesty of her attire now, for she was covered from neck to ankles in black—apart from the wide white collar— with long sleeves closely fitting at the wrist. She had found a freshly laundered cap of plain white linen, which sat neatly on her head, covering it to well below her ears. This was how she habitually dressed to attend church, and even the most ardent of the elders could now have found no fault with her. It won her only a sarcastic twist of a smile from the lips of the Cavalier.

'Egad! I liked you better as you were before.'

She tossed her head angrily, and, refusing the hand he held out to assist her, climbed back to the high seat on the cart. She had no need of his help— at least not to get up into a cart. He appeared not to be in the least put out by her obvious disapproval of his remark. He seated himself beside her, but did not immediately set the horse moving on again.

'In a few minutes' time we shall be within sight of Thickby,' he told her. 'We will go to the Vicarage House, where I am sure you will be well looked after.'

Evidently he knew something about the area, but she thought it wiser not to question him about it. She said, with careful control, determined not to show her emotions, 'I hope we shall find a pastor, for I must arrange to give my father a proper Christian burial.'

'I shall make arrangements for that as soon as we reach the village.' He spoke with compassionate practicality.

The track was skirting the edge of the wide field, with a high hedge along the side and across the far end. Suddenly a group of horsemen appeared, trotting round a corner, dust from the dry ground swirling around them.

'God's blood! Roundheads.' Edward's exclamation was one of alarm. Momentarily he checked the mare.

The riders, about twelve in number, were approaching fast. They came at a canter, dust swirling up from the pounding hooves. Already the little wagon must have been seen, and there was no way they could avoid meeting with the horsemen. Prudence felt the tension in Edward's body as he sat stiffly upright. She saw alertness gouge deep lines in his face. For him, these men, whose horse's hooves beat an ever-louder tattoo as they drew nearer, spelt danger. Suddenly he reached behind him, fumbled into the back of the wagon, brought out Jacob's high-crowned, broad-brimmed black hat and jammed it on to his own head. He set the horse ambling forward again. There was even the semblance of a wry grin as he turned towards her.

'Will I pass as a good Puritan, Prudence?' he asked. His eyes held hers with a query, and immediately she knew what he was asking. Would she help him to play the part—or denounce him as an impostor?

Normally she would have known no fear of the Oliverian militia—but being with Edward Hayward changed that completely. His danger suddenly became hers. There was no thought in her head but that she must protect him. She did not pause to consider her position—her reaction was instinctive. She looked him up and down with a critical eye. The outlaw's jerkin would certainly pass muster. She lifted his arm and tore away a tell-tale fragment of lace that had escaped his previous assault. His clothes would not give him away—they were sufficiently nondescript—and certainly the hat gave him a sombre air. There was something in his bearing that lacked humility, but nothing would ever alter that, she thought.

'You look well enough,' she said solemnly.

'I am glad to have your approval, my dear Prudence,' he whispered. 'For I think perhaps we shall have to become rather closely related.'

What did he mean by that? She had no time to ask, for a moment later the Roundheads had surrounded the wagon. Hard faces beneath lobster-pot helmets stared at them, betraying not the least vestige of friendliness. They were armed with swords at their sides and horse-pistols in holsters by their saddles.

'Halt,' called the officer, though that was scarcely necessary because their way was quite blocked. His high rank was shown by a sash of tawny orange.

Edward reined in.

'Your names?' demanded the Roundhead.

'I am Edward Hayward, and——' He turned towards her and caught hold of Prudence's hand in a grip that firmly thrust it palm down on the seat between them and held it there. The movement, though sudden, held such a strong warning that she sat frozen. Although her mouth opened slightly, she restrained the gasp that would otherwise have escaped her lips, as she heard him say, firmly and unmistakably, 'And this is my wife, Prudence.'

'Where do you come from?'

'Norwich.'

'Whither are you bound?'

'We are making our way to Harwich to board ship for the New World, but we have met with disaster, sir. We were attacked by outlaws in the woods back there and my dear wife's father was shot. We have his body in the back of the wagon.'

The leader brought his horse closer to peer over Edward's shoulder. 'There is certainly a body there,' he said. He pointed to two of his men. 'Check the back of the wagon.'

They dismounted and roughly pulled some of the tilts aside. 'Just the body of one old man, sir. No malignants hiding.'

Prudence felt the grip of Edward's hand over hers tighten till it hurt, and shared the tension he obviously felt.

'Attacked by outlaws, you say, Master Hayward? Tell me what happened.'

'We were travelling through the wood back there——'

'Not the normal route to Harwich,' interrupted the officer suspiciously.

'We were given wrong directions when we stayed at a country alehouse last night——'

'Where?'

'Er—it was...' Edward floundered.

'The Cross Keys,' Prudence supplied the name for him. She felt the grip of Edward's hand lessen fractionally. By her confirmation she had incriminated herself. Too late now to say 'This man is not my husband—he was not with my father and me last night.'

'I know the place. A hive of evil-doers and a two-faced swine of a landlord. Go on.'

'My father-in-law was driving, with my wife beside him,' said Edward, glibly enough. 'I was riding on the back, when the outlaws burst from the woods...'

Keeping close to the truth, Edward told of the attack and how he had shot one of the outlaws while the other had made off into the woods.

'I left his body at the side of the track for his fellow ruffians to deal with,' Edward finished.

'You saw no one else?'

Edward shook his head. 'There were only the two of them, as far as I could see.'

'No one in the King's uniform?'

'No one—except for those outlaws.'

'You know that anyone shielding malignants will be punished with the utmost severity?'

Prudence trembled at the sternly threatening tone of the officer. Edward's grip on her hand tightened again.

'Quite right, too,' he agreed glibly. 'But we have done no harm and I pray you will allow us to continue on our way so that we may reach some place where I can make the necessary arrangements to give my revered father-in-law a decent Christian burial.'

'All in good time. The village of Thickby lies just beyond those trees. There is a vicar, not entirely of our persuasion, but he will do his duty.' Tension building up in Prudence made the tears well into her eyes and roll gently down her cheeks. She dashed them away with her free hand. The officer remained unmoved and turned his searching gaze on her. 'Do you confirm what your husband says?'

'Yes, sir.'

'We have reason to believe that a noted leader of the Royalists who escaped his proper fate at Preston has come this way.'

'I would have reported him to you immediately if we had encountered any such person,' declared Edward. Prudence guessed he was deliberately trying to draw the questioning away from her.

The officer was not to be deflected. 'I am addressing your wife,' he said. He fixed her with a penetrating eye as he asked, 'Mistress Hayward, are you sure you have encountered no one else on the road back there?'

It was probably fortunate that her face was so stained with tears that it was difficult to read her expression. Lying did not come easily to her, nor did she find it easy to respond to that name, but it was too late to refute it. In a low, steadfast voice she answered quite positively, 'No one else, sir.'

Edward made a movement of impatience as if he would have moved on, but the officer was not finished with his inquisition. He held up a hand. 'Not so fast. There is one more question. You are a man of military age—how is it that you are not with one of the fighting forces?'

'I have done my duty,' Edward Hayward replied. 'I have been in battle.'

'I am glad to hear it,' said the officer. He stared suspiciously into Edward's face. 'What regiment were you in?'

'I saw action with the Eleventh Troop of the Ironsides, sir.'

'Ah-ha.' There were a few chortles of merriment among the men. 'The Maidens' Troop, eh? Serving under Major Swallow?'

'Major Swallow was indeed the commanding officer,' agreed Edward smoothly.

'I understood they were marching northwards in pursuit of the King's forces.'

'You are mistaken, I fear. After routing the King's men, the troop was given leave to return to its home towns and villages to assist with the harvest.'

'God be praised they they won so victoriously.'

Prudence noted that Edward did not reply, only bowed his head, as if in agreement. She was watching closely because his mention of the Maidens' Troop had awakened sad memories. She, together with many other young ladies from Norwich, had contributed money, sold jewellery and gone without pleasures to raise a troop as part of the Eastern Association. It had been a reaction to the tales of horror which had reached them—tales of how Royalist soldiers had ravished the young women in any town that fell to their forces. The rumours had lost nothing in the telling and it was thus believed to be for their own protection that they should help to raise troops for Cromwell.

The memory of Ralph, her beloved brother, riding away with the newly formed troop was still vivid in her mind—she had waved her kerchief gaily, as had the other girls and women. He had never returned. Word had come through to them some three weeks later that he had died of wounds received on the battlefield. That news had started a decline in her father's health, and, although he had seemed to rally, it had been no surprise to Prudence that he had felt utterly defeated when his premises were destroyed in that dreadful night of rioting. Dear God—how would it all end? What would happen to Edward—and to her—if his identity was discovered?

'Good,' said the officer, seeming at last to be satisfied. He backed his horse away slightly and Prudence thought the ordeal was over. Then he added, 'Since you assure us you have seen no one, we may as well turn about and accompany you back to the village.'

CHAPTER THREE

THE Cromwellian officer rode off at the head of his troop.

'I could well do without their company,' Edward muttered. Prudence nodded with understanding, then drew in her breath sharply. There was a distinctly disconcerting twinkle in his eyes as he added, 'But, sweet wife, it seems we have no alternative but to follow them.'

Prudence sat in thoughtful silence, alarmed at what might be the consequence of his declaration—and her tacit acceptance—that they were man and wife. She clenched her hands into tight fists, thinking what a fool she had been not to deny it. And yet how could she? This man beside her, who had lied so convincingly, had saved her from almost certain rape and death—she shuddered with horror at the vividly repulsive recollection of that brute of an outlaw who had mercilessly shot her father. In her mind's eye she could see again the lust in his eyes as he had clawed her down from the wagon.

No. She could have reacted in no other way, for to have disputed the relationship that Edward had proclaimed would certainly have resulted in his arrest. She had no doubt that he was the Royalist officer they were seeking. If they even suspected he was not a Parliamentarian he would be vigorously interrogated and in all likelihood condemned to death. Now it was too late. The Roundhead officer had addressed her as Mistress Hayward, and she had answered to that name. She was deeply caught up in the lie—but where would it lead now? That twinkle in Edward's eyes, coupled with all the stories she had heard of the amorous activities of Royalist courtiers, presented a new and very disturbing threat. He looked relaxed and happy, giving the impression that all danger had been averted— but had it? Did the soldiers suspect, even yet? The least little slip could undermine their precarious position.

She tightened the line of her lips and dared not look at Edward as he flicked the reins over the horse's wide back and set the cart in motion to follow the soldiers. Half an hour later they entered the village and rolled along a narrow street of low white-walled cottages that led into a roughly cobbled market square. At the far end was a small flint church with a thatched roof and narrow circular tower, with a graveyard at one side of it, surrounded by a flint wall.

The Roundhead officer glanced over his shoulder and waved an imperious arm, indicating that they should follow him across the square towards a tall house, also built of flint, and thatched. It sat snugly in a well-tended garden of vegetables and herbs. Beyond it was an orchard where pigs rooted and grunted beneath the trees. In answer to a shout from the officer the door was opened by the pastor, poorly clad in faded brown.

'Mr Kent,' the officer addressed him with due regard to his clerical calling, 'this couple are Master and Mistress Hayward, who have met with great misfortune, and are in need of your services. Mistress Hayward's father has been killed by outlaws.'

'Oh, my dear young lady, I am deeply sorry to hear that.' The pastor's voice was warm and sympathetic. 'Of course, my wife and I will do anything we can——'

'Then I will leave Mistress Hayward in your good hands, Pastor,' the officer interrupted brusquely. 'Master Hayward must come with me to make a report to the Intendent.'

Prudence felt the little knot of fear tighten in her heart—that would mean another inquisition for Edward. Could he—could she—keep on telling lies convincingly? Her anxiety must have shown in her face, though she had tried to conceal it, for Edward placed an arm around her shoulder, and she could almost have believed that he really was concerned for her. The touch seemed to burn into her flesh— she had to pretend that this man was her husband, and therefore more dear to her than any other man on earth. She kept her eyes downcast, not daring to look at him.

'You will be in good hands here, Prudence, and I shall rejoin you shortly.' He spoke as if it were all so ordinary, but it took all her self-control to keep from trembling. Evidently he felt it, for he gave her shoulder a reassuring squeeze. 'Just wait one moment and I'll help you down.'

She could not have moved of her own volition had she tried. She heard the pastor speaking in a sing-song voice that he obviously used from the pulpit. 'Your wife will be perfectly comfortable with us until you return, Master Hayward. I'll call my good lady immediately——'

He had no need to do so, however, for at that moment a short plump lady bustled out of the house. A lacy mob-cap sat slightly askew on her light brown hair, her sleeves were rolled up to the elbows and she was wiping floury hands on a large white apron. The smile of welcome that had been beaming on her round red face changed to sorrowful sympathy as she heard of the tragedy that had befallen these unexpected guests. Prudence took comfort from the friendliness of this homely youngish woman, who voiced her opinions strongly. 'The villains! Oh, what dreadful times we live in! What is the country coming to?'

Edward leapt down from the cart and hurried round to where Prudence was shakily getting to her feet, just managing to keep her shock and grief under control. He held up his arms to assist her and, under the close scrutiny of the pastor and his wife, lowered her carefully to the ground. He kept one arm supportively around her waist, and his hold tightened as she stumbled slightly, for in a flood of pent-up emotion tears began to roll down her cheeks and cloud her eyes. Gently he ushered her towards Mistress Kent.

'My wife is still shocked by what has happened,' he said. 'I pray you to take good care of her.'

'That I will. You come into the house with me, Mistress Hayward.'

'I will join you as soon as I can, Prudence,' Edward said.

She looked up at him through eyes brimming with tears. 'God be with you,' she said fervently.

'Come. Hurry along,' commanded the officer impatiently, his eyes beetling beneath the steel of his helmet. 'The Intendent has set up his office in the church. Leave your horse and cart here, Hayward, and follow me on foot.'

'My lad will stable and feed the animal,' said the pastor.

Edward gave him a brief nod of thanks, his arm dropped from her waist and immediately he strode off, a commanding figure, walking briskly alongside the Roundhead's horse. Anxiously Prudence watched him go—and felt as if a lifeline had been wrenched from her. Would they accept his story? To her, his very bearing revealed that he was Cavalier rather than Parliamentarian. It terrified her to think they might well see that too.

'Do not be alarmed, Mistress. It is only routine—your husband will be back very soon,' the pastor said comfortingly.

'Yes—of course…' She tried to sound convinced.

'Go into the house with my wife,' he advised.

'I—I must see to my father——'

'No, my dear. That is not for you to do. I shall call in a woman from the village. All will be done with proper care.'

She was grateful for that. 'Thank you.' Then she remembered—the box and the key. 'My—my father is wearing a belt—it has a key which I shall need.'

'I will bring it to you.'

'There is also a box—underneath the front passenger-seat——'

'I'll bring it in for you. It will all be perfectly safe.' While he spoke Mr Kent had helped to unharness the horse, and the boy now led the animal forward out of the shafts. 'Give him a good feed,' he instructed.

'Come inside the house with me, Mistress Hayward,' coaxed Mistress Kent. 'I've some new bread rising, ready to go into the oven.'

It would have been ungracious not to comply, and, although Prudence remained a little anxious about the box, she turned immediately, wiping her eyes as she did so. With a great effort she controlled herself enough to produce a watery smile. 'We must not allow the bread to spoil, Mistress Kent. And, I pray you, do not put yourself to trouble over me.' Life had to go on, and, although she could not help grieving over the sudden violent death of her father, she must not inflict her suffering on these friendly people. She was grateful to have such kindly help. A delicious smell of baking greeted her as she entered the kitchen, and the homely cheerfulness of the Kent's home acted as a balm. Mistress Kent ushered her to a chair by the window, at the side of which stood a half-worked tapestry on a frame.

'These are my three children,' Mistress Kent said. Her gaze swept around the kitchen, checking on

the activities of each of her offspring. All were tidily
dressed in small replicas of their parents' clothes,
cheaply dyed in faded blues and browns. A girl aged
about twelve had very efficiently taken over from
her mother, and was energetically kneading dough
on the long scrubbed table. Mistress Kent watched
her critically for a moment, then nodded with smug
satisfaction. 'That's a good girl, Amelia.'

Amelia smiled and bobbed a brief curtsy to
Prudence, then turned back and pounded the dough
even harder. Two younger children, a boy and a
girl, were playing marbles with little balls of baked
clay. They stood up respectfully as their mother
called them to be introduced.

Mr Kent brought in the wide leather belt, into
the back of which canvas pockets had been skil-
fully stitched, and the boy followed him, struggling
under the weight of the heavy wooden box.

'There you are, my dear. Unless you need it tonight I'll put the box over by the wall.'

'Thank you.' She had brought in with her the
bundle that contained her few personal items. It
comforted her to know that the box was safe.

Mr Kent and the boy went outside again.
Prudence asked his wife if there was anything she
could do to help, but her offer was firmly refused,
so she played with the children, joining in their
game of marbles, keeping them amused while the
work of preparing supper continued. A large black
pot hung over the cheerful wood fire. A delicious
aroma of meat and vegetables emanated from it
when Mistress Kent lifted the lid and stirred the
simmering contents with a long-handled wooden

spoon. The last of the dough was rolled into balls to make dumplings and carefully dropped on top.

It seemed to Prudence that a long time passed as she waited anxiously for Edward. The meal was prepared, the table scrubbed clean of flour and set with spoons and platters. The normal routine of the household carried on and she could only sit, worrying, chewing at her bottom lip, her unease increasing with every passing minute. The gentle dusk of evening began to fall.

Then suddenly the door was flung open, Edward ducked under its low lintel and swung into the room. He stood with feet set firmly apart, head flung back and, sweeping the high-crowned black Puritan hat from his head as if it were a be-feathered bonnet, executed a Cavalier bow that somehow managed to take in everyone. Prudence caught the gleam in his eyes and knew that, whatever had been the questions put to him by the Intendent, he had overcome them.

She was startled to find that the sight of him had brought joy to her heart. Her reaction puzzled and rather shamed her—she was acting as if he were one of her own people, when she knew that she had cause to be deeply suspicious of him. But there was no doubt about it: Edward looked well pleased with life. Mistress Kent returned his smile, her face reddened and shiny from her labours by the fire.

'Master Hayward, you're back! Your good lady has been fidgeting with worry about you.'

Prudence caught the mocking amusement that flashed into Edward's face, making one corner of his shapely lips quiver, and felt the colour flame into her face. She kept her eyes downcast, convinced that her whole head, from the neck upwards, must closely resemble Mistress Kent's in redness—and she had no excuse of being too near the fire. She was glad that the good lady appeared not to notice and chattered on, 'You're just in time—the meal is all ready.'

'And delicious it smells, my good lady,' he replied. 'I declare I am quite famished with hunger.'

'Then sit yourself down at once,' ordered Mistress Kent. 'Amelia—draw off a jug of ale. Mary—hand me the platters. Robert—you run and fetch your father.'

'Nay, the good pastor will be here in a moment. I have been talking with him outside,' said Edward. Then his face took on a more sober expression as he crossed the room to where Prudence was sitting close to the window, though little light now came through it. The fire had been stoked to increase its glow and lighten the room.

'All is well?' Prudence asked, scanning his face. Even as she asked the question she could not help but think wryly how strange it was that, although they were on opposite sides in this dreadful Civil War, their fates were now so linked that her safety depended on his.

'Indeed.' He nodded. 'The Intendent asked me to convey his sympathy to you, and he offered his good wishes for the success of our venture to the New World.' His voice was even; she was aware of the irony contained in his words, but that would not be obvious to the others in the room.

'That is good of him,' she said. The pretence had to be maintained.

There was a brief uneasy pause, then Edward said, 'The pastor has made arrangements for your father's burial.'

'When is it to be?' She was pleased that her voice was now under control.

'At first light tomorrow morning.'

She guessed it had been arranged so that they might get on their way as early as possible. 'Thank you,' she said.

Mr Kent came in, and went immediately over to Prudence. He took her hands in his and held them comfortingly. 'Your husband has told you of the arrangements?'

'Yes, thank you.'

'A good woman from the village has wrapped your dear father's body in a winding sheet. All will be done according to the rites of the Church, even though those soldiers use the building as their quarters and prevent us from using it.'

'God is everywhere, my father used to say.'

'Amen to that.'

While they were talking Mistress Kent and her daughters had set steaming platters of meat and vegetable stew with herbs and dumplings on the table, and beside each plate was a tankard of ale. 'Come now. Take your places while the food is hot,' Mistress Kent invited them.

The fresh country food was delicious, and Prudence was surprised to find she was quite hungry. Certainly all the others around the table were eating the meal with obvious appreciation.

Edward lifted his hat in salute to his hostess and raised his tankard. ''Tis a meal fit for a——' Prudence stifled a gasp and he paused. 'Shall we say fit for any commoner in the land?' he declared.

The slight tension that had made everyone stop eating and gaze at him passed. Prudence noted that there had been no hostility in anyone's expression and concluded that these good people were not entirely opposed to King Charles, though with strangers in the house they would have been reluctant to admit it.

'Master Hayward tells me that you wish to move on as swiftly as possible tomorrow,' said Mr Kent.

'Yes. We are on our way to Harwich, to board a vessel bound for New England,' Prudence said.

'Won't you stay here and rest for a few days?' Mistress Kent invited. 'You've had such a shock——'

'It's kind of you, but I—we are behind time already. I fear if we do not meet up with our travelling companions within a day or two we may not get to the port in time, and the ship will sail without us. The onset of winter will probably prevent another sailing before next spring.'

'Such a long journey! I would never have the courage to face life in such primitive conditions.'

'I have an uncle who has been in America for several years and he has long been asking that my father and I should join him. Then when our house and warehouses were burned...'

Prudence explained a little of the circumstances that had finally made them take the risk of setting out. She spoke carefully, thoughtfully, and was at pains to include Edward in the plans.

The room had darkened while they ate. A single candle was lit to allow them to clear the table and clean the platters, then the children were sent off to their beds in the attic rooms, their mother taking the candle to light the way for them. She brought it down with her almost immediately. Candles were expensive and Prudence guessed the family would have to use them frugally—it might indeed be the only one they possessed. She judged that the family normally went to bed early, and, being tired, was quite willing to retire herself.

The bedroom to which Mistress Kent led her was reached by a winding stairway set in the wall beside the fireplace. 'This is Amelia's room,' Mistress Kent explained. 'But she has gone up with the smaller ones into the attic for tonight.'

'I'm sorry to have caused so much upset to your household,' Prudence apologised.

'Think nothing of it,' said her hostess. 'We're well used to accommodating travellers, especially in these dreadful times. And it's been a pleasure to me to have your company, though I am indeed sorry for the trouble that has brought you here. I only hope they catch those outlaws. The country seems to be full of wickedness. It's no longer safe for anyone to venture into the woods around here, especially for women. When we gather herbs and medicinal plants we have to go in a group, and even then we have to ask some of the men to accompany us if we need to go beyond the boundary of the village. But I have no wish to load our troubles on to your young shoulders. I hope you will be comfortable in here, my dear.'

Prudence smiled wearily and looked around the room. It was dominated by a heavy four-poster bed with curtains of a deep shade of pink. Rushes were strewn on the floor and there were tapestry hangings on two walls, while the other had a small glazed window.

'I am sure I shall be very comfortable. You have been most kind.'

'I'll leave you the candle——'

'I can manage without—the moon is getting up quite brightly and shines through this window.'

'If you're quite sure?'

'Most certainly, Mistress Kent.'

'Then I'll take it to light my way down. I'll give it to your husband to bring up with him.'

Prudence swallowed. She sought in vain for some words which might prevent Mistress Kent sending Edward up to her here, but nothing convincing came to her mind. In a moment the good lady had taken the candle and disappeared through the door.

Despite her bold assurance that the moonlight would be sufficient, it took some time for Prudence to adjust her eyes to the darkness. Even when she did, the room seemed to be totally dominated by the large four-poster bed. A beam of moonlight lay tantalisingly across it, highlighting the folds of the feather-stuffed covers with such sensuality that she could not bear to look at them but quickly turned her back and walked to the window and stood there in a state of agitation.

At first she was too disturbed to see anything, but as a cloud was chased away from the moon and its light brightened she was able to make out the tower of the church skirted by some trees. The village was in total darkness, and she assumed that all the cottagers were in their beds, as befitted poor country folk. They would be up early enough in the morning to start their toil in the fields at daybreak.

The peace of the scene ought to have stilled the racing of her heart, but never for a moment did she forget that she was waiting for Edward to come to her. Her ears were strained to catch the slightest sound, the creaking of every beam in the house, the soft whistle made by a gust of wind in the thatch. Half an hour must have passed before she heard the sound of the door at the bottom of the stairs being opened quietly, followed by the tread of feet coming up steadily, nearer and nearer.

The latch clicked as he lifted it. She knew that he was there, on the threshold, though she did not immediately turn round, but stood, straight-backed and stiff, her mind in a turmoil. Edward, whom the good pastor and his wife believed to be her husband, who was an officer in the King's service, a Cavalier with all that implied. She did not trust him at all; only extraordinary circumstances had bound them together—much too closely for her peace of mind. It was one thing to act the part of husband and wife downstairs, among company, but quite a different matter to be faced with him here, alone and in the intimacy of her bedroom.

'Go away,' she spat sharply, spinning round.

He stepped into the room and closed the door behind him.

'Tut-tut,' he said softly. 'That is no way to greet your devoted husband.'

Everything about him was ominous, threatening. She drew back until her spine was pressed hard into the edge of the window-sill. Since she could retreat no further, she was forced to stand her ground, and did so with all the courage she could muster. 'One step further and I'll scream.'

'I think not.' He continued to advance across the room towards her. His eyes, dark hollows in his shadowed face, were fixed relentlessly upon her.

She quivered, opened her mouth, intending to carry out her threat, but her tongue felt dry and seemed to be stuck to the roof of her mouth.

'Scream,' he invited, his voice smooth. 'If anyone comes I shall explain you are having a nightmare, and I shall be obliged to hold you very tightly in my arms until you are comforted.'

'Never.' She spat the word at him so positively that it was almost a sneer. But she had stayed silent too long, listening to him, and now he was so close that he would only need to reach forward to carry out his vile threat.

A moonbeam crossed his face and she saw that he was frowning, tight-lipped: her rejection had angered him and she was glad of it.

'You have no reason for alarm,' he said.

'Then keep your distance.'

'I will, most certainly, when I am assured you will not create a scene.'

'You may as well know I am not accustomed to sharing my bedroom.'

'And you imagine that I am?' The amused tone of his voice did nothing to calm her.

'Yes,' she snapped.

At that a soft chuckle escaped his lips. 'All right—I will admit I am not averse to sharing my bed with a woman, providing she is willing,' he agreed with despicable calm.

She tossed her head. 'If you stay here I shall fight——'

'What a she-cat you are.'

'I shall defend myself——'

He spread his hands innocently. 'Against what? You are as safe here with me as you would be in whatever virginal bower you normally inhabit. I have never taken a woman by force, and I would find no pleasure in doing so, especially not here and now.' His tone was scathing.

She tightened her lips primly, then wished that she had not done so as her action brought a twitch of amusement to the corners of his sensitive mouth.

'I have heard that Puritan maids are by nature cool, reserved, afraid of their own natural appetites,' he murmured.

'And I have heard that Cavaliers are lecherous ravishers,' she was stung to retort swiftly.

Far from angering him, her words deepened the smile that had lifted the corners of his lips, showing his white, even teeth, and again that low chuckle rippled out between them. 'It will be quite fascinating to travel on together and discover which, or indeed if either, of those perceptions is the truth.'

'You may think it old-fashioned and amusing that I cherish my chastity,' she said, and her face burned with embarrassment even as she forced herself to speak of it, 'but I make no apology for holding on to my beliefs, even though it would appear that we have no option but to travel on together.'

'No option whatsoever,' he conceded. His voice was cool, practical, but the laughter lines lingered around his eyes in a way that she found disconcerting.

'I have to concede that I am grateful to have you accompanying me until I meet with the others in the group who are emigrating. But after tonight—when we leave this place—there will be no need for us to keep up this pretence of being man and wife.'

'You find the situation—alarming?'

'No. Intensely annoying,' she snapped.

He sighed. 'Ah! As I feared, you also lack a sense of humour.'

She fumed. It seemed that, no matter what she said, he was determined to make fun of her. 'What I lack at the moment is the privacy to get to my bed,' she retorted.

He moved forward and she stepped quickly aside. 'There is no need to distrust my every movement,' he said. He stood beside her, facing the window. 'I was merely obeying your wish to the best of my ability. I shall stand and gaze out of the window and, as soon as you're in bed——' He paused and her heart began to race alarmingly. Coolly he continued, 'As soon as you're in bed I shall curl up on the mat at your feet.'

'You—you cannot sleep in my room,' she objected.

'Believe me, I would not dream of doing so were it not absolutely imperative. When you are in this mood your company is not the most amiable.' She glowered at him, but he merely smiled back and continued, 'You must agree, however, that both Mr and Mistress Kent would be most surprised if I deserted my sweet young wife.'

'But—but my reputation...' She floundered, finding speech almost impossible, desperate to find a way out of this extremely indecorous situation. 'I—I have my future to think of——'

'We shall neither of us have any future to think of should my identity be discovered, for then it will be obvious that you have been assisting me.'

'I could explain——'

'To those desperadoes?'

'It would go worse for you than for me if you were discovered.'

His eyes narrowed. 'I am not so sure of that. As a young woman you have more to lose than I have.'

'Cromwell's men are of the same persuasion as I am.'

'Don't depend on that to help you. You may take my word for it that soldiers are not so very different, no matter which army they are in. I saw the glances that several of them raked you with.'

She swallowed. The Roundheads would have little sympathy for her. She certainly had no wish to be cross-questioned by them, for she too had been aware of the boldness of scrutiny she had come under. She suddenly realised that she would be more afraid to be alone with some of those men than she was with Edward. Still, she was reluctant to let him see any softening of her rejection of him.

'Very well,' she said curtly. 'But you will sleep on the floor, and stay there until the morning.'

'Like a dog,' he agreed.

Her mouth twitched a little. She could not imagine anyone less like a dog—unless he was a large and handsome hound of immense pride and strength.

'And pray keep your back turned to the bed.'

His lip curled, and she felt his contempt. 'I am a man of honour,' he said. 'I have already assured you, you have nothing to fear from me—this night.'

He stood aside and gave a mocking bow as, with her head held high, she walked past him. It was a coolly polite gesture, but somehow it gave her an uncomfortable feeling that she had been in the wrong. That was totally unfair—it had been he who had been provocative. When she reached the head of the bed she glanced back to satisfy herself that Edward was gazing out of the window, just as he had promised. She hesitated for only a matter of seconds before she unlaced and removed her gown. Her fingers fumbled on the fastenings of her whalebone corset, but once that was off it was the work of moments to untie the strings and step out of her two petticoats. She sat on the edge of the bed to remove her shoes and stockings. Once more she cast an anxious glance to reassure herself that Edward remained as before, very still, with his broad back squarely to the room. Then she pulled her day-shift over her head, replaced it with a night-shift, quickly climbed into the bed, and closed the curtains around her.

'You may lie down now,' she said.

'I thank you, gracious lady,' he said with heavy sarcasm.

She heard the soft thump as he dropped down on to the rush mat at the foot of the bed. How hard it must be, lying there, especially for one who was obviously used to more luxurious living! Well, that just serves him right, she thought. He should never have made that wild assertion that they were man and wife—why couldn't he have said brother and sister? She heard a louder thump as he removed his heavy boots, then restless movements. Curled in the soft depths of the warm feather bed, she could not prevent a feeling of sympathy for him.

'This may help,' she called, and as she did so lifted one of her pillows and hurled it through the bed-curtains.

'Why—the lady has a heart after all,' he murmured.

Presently there was stillness in the room. Prudence did not expect to sleep easily—the events and dangers of the day were too close—but in a surprising way she felt comfort and safety in the knowledge that Edward was there, in the room with her. With the bed-covers pulled up close under her chin, it was not long before nature forced her to close her eyelids, and she drifted into oblivion.

CHAPTER FOUR

WHEN Prudence awoke she lay for a moment wondering where she was, then all the events of the previous day flooded back into her mind. The violent death of her father was still a shocking grief, but she comforted herself by saying a prayer and reminding herself that he was now at peace and in the hands of God, whom he had served so well all his life.

She thanked God too for keeping her safe through the night, then, still shielded by the bed-curtains, she listened for any sound from the room. All was silent. Where was Edward? She crawled down to the foot of the bed and stealthily raised one corner of the drapes. The pillow she had flung out lay on the floor, indented where a head had rested, but there was no sign of the Cavalier. She drew in a deep breath of relief, but her concern remained. Being in the Christian household among the Kent family had undoubtedly given her sanctuary through the night—but what threats and dangers lay ahead today?

Whatever they were, she felt refreshed and prepared to face them. She was surprised that she had slept so soundly and well. She must keep her wits about her as they travelled on, for she acknowledged that until they reached up with the rest of the emigrating group it would be necessary for her to remain with Edward. Better the devil she knew than any that she didn't, she thought wryly. She slipped out of her night-shift, but before she had time even to pull her day-shift over her head she heard the tread of footsteps on the stairs, and moved swiftly to hide behind the drapes of the bed. The steps halted at the door. There was a soft rapping, and the door was opened.

'Mistress Hayward—I've brought you some warm water.' With relief and pleasure Prudence realised it was Amelia.

'Thank you. That is very kind.' With all possible speed she began to don her underwear.

'Shall I pour it into the bowl for you?'

'Please. Am I very late, Amelia?'

'Not at all. It is only just after dawn. Master Hayward came down only a few minutes since. Breakfast will be ready shortly.'

After a refreshing wash, Prudence finished dressing and brushed out her long golden hair which was always so difficult to subdue. It had an immodest tendency to wave and curl, making it difficult to restrain into a suitably severe head-hugging style. Ruthlessly she tugged at it, gathered it together and screwed it into a bun at the nape of her slender neck as tightly as its natural unruliness would allow. There was no mirror, but she was not accustomed to using one, for that would have suggested vanity. Then, smoothing down the folds of her skirt, she descended to the kitchen.

The table was set with platters of cold salted meat, bread and jugs of home-brewed beer. Prudence looked around for Edward, but neither he nor Mr Kent was there. The younger children were sitting side by side on her wooden box, squabbling as they tried to push each other off. Prudence smiled at them, reassured to see that her box was safe, for, although it was occasionally kicked accidentally, it was strong enough to withstand such treatment. Mistress Kent's round red face beamed a welcome.

'Good morning, Mistress Hayward. Did you sleep well?'

'I did indeed, and I feel much better for it. Can I help you with anything?'

'No—no, my dear. Everything is ready. We are just waiting for my husband and yours to return.'

She did not put it into words, but Prudence guessed that the two men had gone to the churchyard to make arrangements for the burial. There was a small silence, broken when one of the boys wailed pathetically, 'I'm hungry.'

'Hush,' admonished his mother. 'Your father will be here shortly.'

At that moment the door opened and Edward ducked as he passed beneath the lintel, ushered into the room by Mr Kent, and followed by the boy. At once the children rushed to the table, and kindly Mr Kent, understanding their hunger, gathered everyone around and said a brief grace so that they could all sit down, the children on a long bench and the adults on chairs. Naturally Edward and Prudence were seated beside each other, and with the utmost politeness he offered the platter of meat for her to select from.

'No, thank you,' she said. 'I shall just take some bread.'

'Come, Prudence, I know this is a trying time for you, but you must eat,' he said.

'I am not hungry.'

An expression of exasperation brought a scowl to his handsome face. 'We have a long journey ahead of us, and you will need all the strength you can muster if we are to catch up with the rest of the group.'

'I assure you, I am perfectly well and although I am small I am stronger than most women.'

'I do not doubt it.' His voice suggested it was not a trait that he much admired. 'But that does not mean you can travel on an empty stomach.'

She caught a note of annoyance in his tone, and guessed that he was afraid that she might faint and become an encumbrance to him.

Mistress Kent leaned across the table towards her. 'Your husband is right, my dear. You must try to eat, even though you may not really wish to. If you do not fancy the meat, just try a slice of this oatmeal pudding—I made it myself only yesterday.'

Prudence could not refuse her kindness and forced herself to munch some of the good wholesome food. It was indeed so tasty that she managed to consume the whole slice, at which Mistress Kent nodded with pleasure and satisfaction.

'I'll wrap the rest of the pudding in a cloth and you must take it with you to eat on your journey,' she said, and would brook no refusal.

With that and seeing that she had also sipped a little of the small beer, even Edward seemed to be satisfied.

It was mid-morning when Prudence and Edward set off again. The Kent family assembled outside the tall thatch-roofed parsonage to bid them God-speed on their journey, and waved them off with warm good wishes. Prudence was seated on the little wagon and Edward led the horse as they moved away, across the square, leaving behind the church with its bravely upstanding flint tower.

Soon after breakfast the body of her beloved father had been laid to rest in a sunny corner of the peaceful churchyard, where the rooks cawed overhead in the old elm trees. The grave had been dug the previous evening and the vicar had intoned the service in a gentle and caring manner. A woman from the village had wrapped the body of Jacob Collins in a woollen winding sheet. She had bundled together such of his personal effects as had not been completely ruined by his wound, and Edward had placed them in the wagon. All that could be done had indeed been done.

The body of the outlaw had been brought into the village and identified as a wanted murderer and robber, and there was praise for Edward for having disposed of such a dangerous character. It was be-lieved that this man came from the neighbouring village, so the overseer had sent the body there for burial to avoid that expense falling on his parish.

Edward walked as they moved along the village street where cottages clung in neighbourly fashion close together on either side, interspersed with the sheds and yards of tradesmen. The blacksmith's fire glowed red, a labourer held a heavy horse, waiting for it to be shod. The cobbler sat at his window, working at his last. In the carpenter's yard a tree trunk was balanced over the saw-pit, and the man at the top moved up and down as regularly as clockwork, while the hard-worked boy beneath was lost to sight in clouds of falling sawdust. The ale-house was already open but not doing much trade, for most of the villagers were again out in the open fields, making the most of the good weather to reap their harvest.

Soon the village was left behind, the fields gave way to woodland, and beyond this lay a stretch of arid heathland, across which the rutted road stretched into the distance. The false information which her father had been given by the criminal landlord had taken them several miles out of their way, but now, once more, they were travelling in the right direction, towards the town of Tillington. It was there that Prudence expected to meet up with some of the other members of the party which was emigrating. She also had the address of a prominent Parliamentarian who lived in the town; she was confident that he would have information about the rest of the party, and that she could call on him for help if need be.

Once out of the village, Edward left the head of the horse, climbed up into the wagon beside Prudence and took up the reins. 'Do you know any of these people who are emigrating?' he asked.

'I know the names of some, and have met one man, Elias Smith, and his wife, who came to speak to my father about the expedition,' she told him. 'The Smiths have four young children, and believe they will have a better chance of a good life in the New World.'

'Provided they survive,' Edward answered grimly.

'That is in the hands of God,' Prudence reminded him. 'But it can hardly be worse than what is happening in this country, for the King does nothing but raise taxes to fight wars in foreign lands, instead of looking after his own people here properly.'

'King Charles has his faults,' said Edward, 'but he is by no means bad. He is a shy man really.'

'Do you know him?'

'I have met him. I like him. I would rather entrust the country to his hands than those of Oliver Cromwell.'

'He is deluded when he thinks that he has been chosen by God to be the King of England.'

'And how do you know that he has not?' Edward asked.

'I think God would have chosen a better man for the task,' she replied.

'Not Oliver Cromwell!' Edward said in a voice of such fierce authority that she drew back from him a little. 'Never that villain!'

'That we shall see,' she replied with a quiet, firm dignity.

She sat very upright, looking straight in front of her. His explosive words reminded her of how little they had in common. She worried how best to cope with those differences—their loyalties, their beliefs, their moral values were utterly opposed, yet they were forced into travelling together. She knew that on her own she would be in grave danger of another ambush by robbers and she was grateful for the protection that Edward's presence gave her. When it came to dealing with outlaws he was strong and fearless.

She had no wish to emphasise their enmity—she was far too spirited to endure his criticisms without a strong desire to answer back; however, common sense told her she must try to establish a truce of some sort between them. It most certainly would not be in the interest of either of them to spend their day arguing, especially as neither would be likely to give way. It was, as he had admitted, as much to his advantage as it was to hers that they should be together. On his own Edward would have had difficulty in hiding his true identity as a Royalist officer—a gentleman whose name was on the wanted list of every Roundhead troop.

'Master Hayward,' she said, determined to break the silence which had fallen between them, 'until we reach Tillington, and maybe beyond, we have need of each other's company. Could we not make a pretence at least of amiability?'

'Nothing would please me better,' he responded at once. 'But I have one serious reservation: are you capable of regarding me in a kindly light?'

She bit her lip to control a rising anger, and sat staring straight ahead as if fascinated by the outline of a little low building they were approaching. It was no use pretending she approved of him, for she was convinced he was lacking in morals. All Cavaliers were. 'Sir, I try most positively to maintain kindly feelings towards all human beings, but I have to confess that I find it easier with some than with others.'

They came nearer to the building, an ale-house strategically situated at a crossroads, and still he remained silent. She began to wonder whether she had spoken too rashly, though she felt no compunction, for her answer had been no more than he deserved. The trouble was that, far from holding out a hand of friendship as she had intended, her honesty had made her speak more bluntly than she should have.

'Then I fear you will just have to continue the struggle,' he said, his voice even and unemotional. 'For we are bound closely together as man and wife, are we not?'

'You know we are not,' she replied sharply. 'There is no necessity for that charade to continue now that we are away from those who were told such lies.'

'A minor fabrication,' he said dismissively. 'And may I remind you it was one with which you fully concurred.'

'Not fully,' she objected. 'I had no choice.'

'And you have no choice now.' His voice was steely. 'So long as we travel together it will be expedient that we should present ourselves as a devoted and loving couple.'

'No. I will not be drawn deeper into this maze of deceit. There is no need——'

'On the contrary, my dear Prudence, I assure you that, for the safety of both of us, if we travel together we must continue as we are now.'

'I will not,' she said angrily between clenched teeth. 'My honour will not allow it a moment longer. I will not be presented as your wife when we reach Tillington.'

'That is definite?'

'Absolutely.'

'Very well.'

To her amazement he handed her the reins, and leapt off the wagon. 'Then fare thee well, Prudence Collins.' He gave the horse a hearty slap on the rump and strode off towards the ale-house and before she could recover from her astonishment had disappeared inside.

The horse, disconcerted by the sharpness of the slap, had broken into a canter, a ragged movement which Prudence controlled only with difficulty. Pulling hard on the reins, she forced the affronted animal to slow and eventually to walk. She glanced back over her shoulder; there was no sign of Edward so she had to conclude, reluctantly, that he'd meant what he'd said.

The ale-house had been an isolated building at a crossroads in desolate moorland countryside. The signpost pointed to Tillington, so she knew she was travelling in the right direction, but she felt distinctly reluctant to continue on her own. Ahead was a thicket of trees—who knew what or who might be lurking there? The sky was darkening behind it, increasing its sinister appearance. She shuddered, and a tear pricked behind her eyelids, forcing her to acknowledge her weakness. She fancied again that she could see a shaking in the undergrowth, just as she had done only yesterday, when the robbers had leapt out on her and her father. How could Edward be so cruel as to desert her here?

'Whoa. Whoa, there.' She pulled the horse to a standstill, and sat and struggled hard with herself, trying to convince herself that she could manage. But the truth was inescapable—she simply had not the courage to travel on alone. Everything she had thought of him was confirmed—he was even more selfish and overbearing than she had imagined. Any good she had seen in him was overshadowed by anger at the way he had abruptly abandoned her, and at that moment she disliked him intensely— hated him, even though that was an unchristian sentiment. She lifted the reins, and tried again to muster enough courage to drive on alone, but she could not.

The lowering sky was forbidding, the thicket ahead threatening and impenetrable. Reluctantly she knew she was beaten. Whatever conditions Edward imposed, she would have to agree to them, but it would not be for much longer, she promised herself fiercely. If Edward did not linger in the ale-house and they kept going they would reach Tillington before dark, then with luck they would meet up with the rest of the convoy. Once she was with her own people her worries would be over. She could then part company from this arrogant, selfish brute—and it would not be a moment too soon. Now she must swallow her pride and try to placate him—temporarily, at least.

Having made this decision, she flipped the reins on to the horse's back, turned the animal around and walked it steadily back to the ale-house. She looped the reins up carefully, then stepped down and walked to the low door, roughly constructed of knotted planks. There she hesitated. It was a common ale-house, which she had been warned was a den of iniquity, and she had never in her life entered such a place. Uncertain of etiquette, she knocked lightly on the door and waited. Laughter came from within, rough guffaws, which did nothing to bolster her courage.

No one answered the door, so she lifted the latch, pushed it open and stepped over the threshold. A haze of smoke from a peat fire lay over the dusky interior, which was decidedly short of windows, and, by the general reek that met her nostrils, those that were there had not been opened in a decade. She stared around and spotted Edward quickly enough. He was seated on a hard wooden settle, his legs thrust out before him, a tankard of ale in his hand, absorbed in conversation with an old countryman. He looked up as she entered, took a draught of ale and wiped the froth from his lips with the back of his hand as roughly as any peasant.

'Ah! Here she comes! Women! Never allow a man to enjoy a measure in peace, always chasing after 'im. Who'd be married?'

Prudence was disgusted by Edward's behaviour, and could only stare at him, wide-eyed, not daring to react to it as sharply as she would have liked. Her instinct was to turn on her heel and march straight out, to leave him there—yet she knew she must not do that. She could only stand rooted to the spot. Edward turned back to his unsavoury companion, and resumed conversation with him.

In desperation she found her voice. 'Edward— please.' It was little more than a whisper. She thought at first he would ignore her.

Then he looked across in her direction. 'Wait outside, wife,' he growled roughly. 'I'll join you shortly.'

The abrupt command did nothing to appease her, but she obeyed quickly enough, glad to retreat from the stuffy unfriendly atmosphere. The horse had found a tuft of grass by the roadside and was grazing contentedly. She sat down on a wooden bench by the ale-house wall and waited, relieved that at least Edward had not rejected her approach. It was only a few minutes before the door swung open and he strode out through it and stood there, looking such a pillar of strength that immediately, and in spite of everything, she felt her spirits lift.

He looked not at her, but up at the sky. 'It's going to rain,' he announced, his voice cool but friendly. 'We'd better waste no more time.'

She bit back the retort that it was he who had caused time to be wasted, jumped to her feet and marched over to the little wagon. Straight-backed, with her head held high and every line of her fluid body tautened to register disapproval, she clambered up to take her seat. In a moment Edward was there beside her and at once he set the horse moving ahead, urging the willing animal to the fastest pace of which it was capable.

'Interesting old man, that,' Edward remarked conversationally.

She felt no inclination to answer. She cared nothing for the old man, and had no wish to appear more subservient than was strictly necessary, even though Edward had won his point. The first drops of rain were beginning to fall.

'Yes,' Edward said, maddeningly carrying on just as if she had agreed with him. 'He was a valuable source of information about the area.'

Prudence shrugged, displaying her indifference. There was a short period of silence. Then Edward added, 'No one passes this way without his knowing.'

Suddenly her interest quickened. She turned her head sharply and swept his face with her eyes. His benign expression emphasised what his voice had told her—his good humour was completely restored, and there was even a slight smile playing at the corner of his lips. She wished she could feel the same, but she remained furious at her own weakness, chafing at her reliance upon him. He had gleaned some information—that was certain. He was teasing her with it—she could wait no longer. 'What did he say?' she asked.

'Ah, I thought you might be interested.'

'Of course I am,' she snapped.

'A convoy of six wagons with about thirty men, women and children passed this way yesterday. They were on their way to Tillington.'

Her excitement mounted. 'Then we shall meet up with them there.'

'Let us hope so,' Edward replied.

'Surely there is no doubt about that?' The rain was falling harder. She pulled her linen cap forward and caught her cloak more closely around her.

'It was early in the morning when the convoy passed. Over twenty-four hours ago. The old man thought they would most probably be well beyond there by now.'

'Oh.' Her disappointment was intense. The rain was pouring down her face. The ruts and potholes in the road were rapidly filling with muddy water. It was no time for fast travel.

'Have no fear, Prudence,' he said. 'I'll wager we'll catch up with them before the ship sails.'

The wagon jolted as it ran into a particularly deep hole in the road. The horse had to strain to keep it going, and Edward jumped down and walked at the animal's head, leading it to avoid the worst of the terrible ruts and puddles. Both Edward and Prudence were rapidly becoming soaked to the skin.

'Shall we reach Tillington tonight?' she shouted at him.

'No. That won't be possible in this weather, but I know of a small village, a couple of miles along the road, where there is an inn. We shall have to put up there for the night.'

An hour earlier Prudence would have argued that they should keep going rather than stay at a remote country place when there was hope of reaching Tillington. Now she was getting wetter with every turn of the wheels. Rain was pouring from her drenched and crumpled cap, running down the neck of her clothes in icy rivulets, soaking her to the skin. She began to shiver uncontrollably as the cold seemed to seep right into her bones; whatever the inn was like, it would be a welcome refuge.

Edward was striding through the rain, encouraging the horse to keep going, guiding it, never stopping for a moment, even though sometimes his boots were deep in mud and puddles. He leaned his strong muscular trunk into the storm without hesitation, taking care to make the horse's task as easy as he could in such terrible conditions. Despite her dislike of him, she had to admire his fortitude and the strength of character that he displayed in such trying circumstances. She had also to admit how fortunate it was for her that he was there. If only he had been of a different persuasion! If only his morals were as strong as his physique!

At last the wagon was trundling through a village street, where the worst of the potholes had been infilled with broken stones, and she could see the hostelry ahead through the veil of rain which poured down relentlessly. Edward led the horse into the yard, and an ostler emerged from a line of wooden stables. 'I'll take care of yer 'oss, sir,' he offered.

'Rub her down well, and give her a good feed. She's earned it.'

'Tis no day even fer a dog ter be out,' agreed the ostler, taking over.

Prudence stretched her cold muscles into movement and began to clamber down. At once Edward was there to assist her and usher her into the house. They entered through the back door, straight into the kitchen, where the warmth and delicious smell of roasting and baking gave a heart-lifting welcome. This was reiterated verbally by the landlord, a plump red-faced advertisement for good living, who had been standing with his back to the fire when they entered.

His wife, rolling pastry on the scrubbed table, smiled in their direction and continued with her work. 'There. I must have known we'd have company tonight. There'll be a fresh-baked pork pie for supper and vegetables straight from the garden.'

The hospitality of the inn could not have been bettered. A fire was soon blazing in a comfortable bedroom, and a maidservant helped Prudence to remove her wet clothes and took them away downstairs to dry. She returned almost immediately with a pitcher of hot water and two large towels.

'Will you need any help, ma'am?' she asked.

'No, thank you. You may go.'

At once Prudence began to wash herself down, scrubbing vigorously, and soon felt her circulation restored, her skin cleansed, dried and rubbed to glowing warmth. She was kneeling by the fire, wrapped only in a towel, drying her long golden hair, when Edward's voice called from outside the door.

'I've brought up your box and some dry clothes, Prudence.'

She hesitated only a moment to make sure that she was completely enveloped in the towel before answering, firmly and clearly, 'Come in.'

He carried her box, and folded on top of it lay a small pile of garments. 'I did not know what you would wish for, so I brought a selection,' he said as he entered. Then he broke off abruptly, staring at her, and there was no mistaking the sensual admiration that leapt into his eyes. She turned away quickly, felt colour flare into her cheeks, and hoped he would think it was caused by the heat of the fire.

'Thank you. Please be so good as to put them down on the floor.' She managed to make her voice sound coolly matter-of-fact.

She heard him move, looked up again and saw that he had done exactly as she had asked and was about to leave the room. Guiltily she noticed that he was still in his soaking outdoor clothes, the water from his hair dripping on to the rushes at his feet.

'You should get changed too,' she said.

'I will.' There was disturbing mischief in the look he shot at her. 'But I thought you would prefer to get dressed before I came in to perform my ablutions.' All the uncertainties she had experienced the previous night returned, augmented by the knowledge that there was no escape from the false position of pretending to be the wife of this man whose vitality seemed like a tangible pulse in the room, so powerful that it threatened to overwhelm her.

CHAPTER FIVE

As soon as Edward had withdrawn and closed the door Prudence dressed with all possible speed, brushed out her hair and, even though it was not quite dry, twisted it back again into its customary tight knot at the nape of her neck. When she opened the door and stepped out of the room Edward was leaning nonchalantly against the wall.

He straightened, raising his eyebrows eloquently at her prim Puritan garb, and she definitely heard a chuckle as with a swift but courteous bow he swept past her and into the bedroom. Before closing the door he said, 'I've arranged a private room in which we can dine. Pray wait there for me, Prudence. I shall not be long.'

The room was very small and intimate, lit by a couple of candles and the glow from a blazing log fire. A spotless white cloth had been spread over a small table, set for two, on which stood a basket of bread and an earthenware jug. Prudence sniffed at the contents, confirming her fear that it was wine. She enjoyed a glass on the odd occasion, but resolved to be wary of it this evening, warning herself that she must not allow her head to become muzzy.

Presently Edward joined her, and almost immediately the landlady came in, bearing a huge meat pie, followed by the maidservant with steaming dishes of vegetables. The savoury aroma set Prudence's mouth watering, reminding her how hungry she was. Soon they were both eating with enjoyment, which for a short time lessened the tension that had gripped her since they had arrived at the inn.

Edward poured wine into the goblets for both of them, and raised his glass to her. 'A toast to the success of our journey together.' She could not refuse to join him in that sentiment, and sipped the wine. It was cool and delicious.

'The landlord keeps a good cellar,' observed Edward.

'I would not know about that. But his wife is certainly a very good cook.'

'Excellent,' he agreed. 'It was fortunate that fate brought us here, for there is no establishment as good as this in Tillington.'

'You have been in this area before?' she questioned.

'I know it a little,' he replied guardedly.

She was curious, and wished, as she had done several times before, that she knew more about him. Past experience made her cautious over questioning him, however, and she contented herself with asking, 'Do you know how far it is to Harwich from here?'

'Two days' travel, if the roads are passable,' he answered immediately, revealing that he really did know the area quite well. 'Twice as long if conditions remain as they have been today.'

A blast of wind-driven rain rattled on the windowpane. 'It still sounds fierce,' she commented.

'I think it will have passed over by daylight—
there are many hours before then.'

His words brought little comfort. She was very
well aware of those hours of the night that they
must pass in embarrassingly close proximity. She
was thankful that throughout the meal Edward
conducted himself in an entirely courteous and
decorous manner, and despite her reservations she
began to relax a little. She even finished her goblet
of wine, and, although she demurred when he lifted
the jug to refill it, she ended up by accepting, 'Just
a little.'

The main course was followed by a syllabub,
richer and creamier than she had ever tasted before,
and so delicious that she quite forgot that one of
its main ingredients was wine. Conversation flowed
between them. Prudence, with her customary
openness, readily answered all the questions he plied
her with, but she could not help noticing that he
told her very little about himself. Certainly the good
food and wine had induced a convivial atmosphere
of companionship between them. The time passed
quickly and happily, until her eyelids began to
droop as she sat at ease with her elbow on the table
and her head propped up on her hand.

Edward noticed and pushed back his chair. 'I
think you are tired,' he said, quite gently.

She nodded. 'I am a little—it has been a long
day.' An age seemed to have passed since they had
left the parsonage at Thickby.

'To bed, then,' he said, rising to his feet.

She looked into his coolly smiling face and con-
gratulated herself that, despite the wine, her brain

was perfectly clear. Unconsciously she tilted her head a little to one side and asked, 'The same sleeping arrangements as last night?'

'Whatever you wish.' He sounded amused.

It aggravated her that he took everything so lightly, for that was not the way she had been taught to look at life. She stood up, and at once he was by her side, offering his arm. 'Allow me to escort you.'

Naturally she had to accept; they were supposed to be man and wife, so she must play her part in the farce to the best of her ability. She smiled up at him, congratulating herself again on being totally in control of the situation. Why was it, then, that when they reached the landing that led to the bedroom her hand trembled as it lay in the crook of his arm? She snatched it away, then stumbled on a rough floorboard and felt angry with herself. It was the wine, of course—she should have refused to take any!

At once his arm closed around her waist, holding her tightly to his side as he steadied her. He opened the bedroom door and guided her through, and, although she would have liked to pull herself away from his hold, she felt unable to do so. Inside the room, he kicked the door shut with his foot, turned her towards him and, still clasping her to him, he lifted her face with his free hand. The firm but gentle pressure of his fingers forced her to look up into his eyes, and she quailed as she read desire in his expression.

'You know you are a very lovely young woman, don't you, Prudence?' he said.

'N-no——' she stammered. 'No——'

'Yes,' he corrected. 'You try to hide your beauty under those unbecoming garments, and by raking your glorious hair back and twisting it into an ugly shape—but you cannot disguise your eyes. There is something in them that calls enticement to a man, but you know that, don't you?'

'No.' Her voice was firmer now, though her body felt as weak and defenceless as ever. 'It's not true. I do nothing——'

'You do not need to. The woman in you is there, crying out——'

With that he caught a raw nerve. 'No!' She shouted the word in fury. It was not she who enticed men—it was men who preyed upon her. She had fought—and would fight again—to keep her purity. She sought for the right words to express her feelings. Before she could find them he bent his head and his mouth closed over hers.

His kiss was unhurried, deliciously long and close, warm and sensual; his lips moved over hers, and with a firm pliancy that awakened emotions she had only dreamed of before that moment. He kissed her with experience, with the erotic knowledge of a man of the world. He deliberately used his expertise to arouse her, pressing her slender young body against his, making her aware of the magic of her femininity, so that her waist seemed fragile, encircled by the strength of his arm.

For several long, lingering minutes it seemed as if she was helpless in his grasp, that she must succumb, and she felt that her whole world depended upon her clinging to him. Her mouth rejoiced in the taste of his—but then that part of her which had been trained to resist overcame his magnetism. Her mind triumphed. She was acting like a hoyden, she told herself severely. Where was her pride? How could she stand there allowing herself to be kissed in such a sensual fashion by this degenerate reprobate? And it was worse to have kissed him back. Anger rose sharply in her and she drew her face back, away from the blandishment, the sweetness of his kiss.

At once he, too, lifted his head. He kept his arms around her, but it seemed to be more to steady her than in an embrace. From a little less than arm's distance they gazed at each other.

'How dare you?' she spat at him.

He remained unabashed. 'There is not much that I will not dare.' It might have been a warning. 'Especially if the prize is worth the winning.'

'I will never be won by you,' she told him.

'I wonder,' he murmured in a thoughtful tone, and his gaze roved over her. 'You dress like a Puritan, and speak like one——' he paused and his eyes met and held hers '—but your thoughts are by no means always as prudish and strait-laced as you would like them to be.'

'How do you know my thoughts?' she snapped at him. The flame of anger in her was fanned because his observation was too near the truth for comfort. She knew it was a disgraceful fault that she had far more sensual thoughts than any good Puritan maiden ever should.

'How do I know?' he mocked. 'Your lips told me, and the sway of your body in my arms—there was no need for words.'

Shame threatened to overwhelm her. She knew exactly what he meant—and recognised that her danger was increased because he was beginning to know her too well. For her own safety she had to refute that idea immediately. She had to separate herself from him, not only physically but mentally too.

'I had rather be a Puritan than one of your kind,' she declared. In fear and fury the words spilled out. 'You are vile, unspeakable... you had no right to take advantage like that, just because you gave me too much wine——'

'It was not the wine that brought communion between us,' he said, and smiled in that infuriating way he had.

'It was certainly nothing else.'

'You think not? I know what I experienced, and those delightful sensations should not be spurned—but we will not quarrel about it.'

'Good.' She glared at him.

Although the smile still hovered around his lips, his eyes met hers coolly. She remained agitated, wringing her hands.

'Poor Prudence—you know so little of life.' She could hardly believe her ears when he added, 'One day, I think, it will be my privilege to teach you.'

'I need no mentor——'

'That we shall see—but at a different place, in a different mood.'

'My feelings towards you will never change.'

Infuriatingly he laughed at that. Then with a shrug of total indifference he turned to the door. 'Meanwhile I shall seek some more amenable company down in the taproom.' He paused on the threshold. 'Rest assured that you will not be troubled again by me.'

As he was about to close the door she called after him, 'I will put the pillow on the floor for you.' There should be no doubt as to where she expected him to sleep.

He bowed. 'My heartfelt thanks, gracious lady.' His voice was heavy with sarcasm as he closed the door gently behind him.

It was some time before her anger and confusion calmed. Automatically she prepared for bed, then paced up and down the room, her emotions still highly charged and her lips tender from Edward's kiss. No man had ever treated her so, and her mind turned over and over all those things that he had said about her. It reminded her forcefully how her father had warned her against vanity, had counselled her never to 'flaunt' herself before men. Now Edward had suggested something of the same thing. It was not true. She did not consciously set out to seek men's attentions. In fact, it was the very reverse—she had deliberately tried to keep her relationship with Edward as remote as their false status allowed.

The position she found herself in was impossible. He was so charming—but she could not, *must* not trust him. There was simply no way she could avoid being with him. Edward had demonstrated that convincingly when he had walked out on her earlier in the day. Not until they met up with the rest of the group with which she would be sailing to America would she be able to put an end to this charade of being man and wife. It had been re-assuring to learn that the convoy was moving along only a day or two ahead of them. Undoubtedly they would meet up at Harwich.

She closed her eyes and prayed that the ship would not sail before they got to port. She felt comforted after that, and able to think more clearly. Edward had promised that he would not trouble her again—and when she thought about it she dis-covered that she trusted him to keep his word. His ardour had been quickly controlled, though not quenched, she knew, but it had been with an air of cool indifference that he had left 'to seek some more amenable company'. His lifestyle was insincere, hollow; he bore no loyalty, except to his King. She would make sure that she kept herself distant from him in the future. Yet the excitement his kiss had awakened could not be easily forgotten. She lifted her hand and lightly brushed her fingers over her lips in wonder, and a strange shiver ran down her whole body. Hastily she reminded herself of the wickedness of such feelings, that this sensual in-volvement of mind and body was not right for a chaste young woman, and in her mental agony she almost groaned aloud.

Would her peace of mind and spirit ever return? Somehow goodness had to triumph—she made a great effort to calm herself. She threw herself on to the bed, pulled the coverlet closely over and deliberately pushed those disturbing recollections to the back of her mind.

When Edward came into the room she listened to his movements and feigned sleep; only when there had been silence in the room for some considerable time did she drift away.

They were on the road again early the following morning. Their clothes had been dried, the horse well-rested and fed, and the sun shone brightly. It was a morning when all should have been well with the world, but there was a definite air of constraint between Prudence and Edward. Her resolve to keep herself as distant from him as was politely possible seemed to be echoed in his treatment of her. He spoke little as they breakfasted, helped her up into the wagon without a smile, and drove along with a taciturn expression on his handsome face.

That should have pleased her, but quite ridiculously it had the opposite effect. She felt depressed. She told herself it was simply a natural reaction to all that had happened, but that did not help her to overcome it. She had no wish to break the silence, but sat with stoical patience, looking beyond the steadily rolling movement of the horse's rump to the narrow dusty road ahead.

It was market day in Tillington, and pigs, sheep and cattle were penned in the square in the centre of the town. Chickens, ducks and geese were tied by their legs; farmers' wives were selling eggs, butter, cakes, apples and herbs. A wandering tinker offered to mend pots and pans, and a basket-maker called out that he would make a skep as big or little as you wished. The bustling, lively, noisy scene awoke Prudence out of her lethargy, and she began to gaze around with interest. Inevitably their progress had to slow right down as they threaded their way among the people and animals.

'Can we find the house of my father's business acquaintance?' Prudence asked. 'His name is Ebenezer Mileham and he lives near the church.'

'I would prefer not to stop here,' Edward said.

She was surprised by the note of anxiety in his tone, and saw that his face was tense, but she shrugged that thought away. He had looked like that for most of the morning, and it was now midday.

'Master Mileham may have news of the convoy,' she persisted. 'I remember my father giving them the address, and telling Master Smith that he might be able to help them on their journey.'

'We do not need his help,' said Edward.

He was being deliberately awkward and obstructive, decided Prudence. In her opinion they needed all the assistance they could get, and she was determined to see Master Mileham if it was at all possible, thought she had only a vague recollection of the man. It was five or six years since he had visited her father, but they had corresponded and done business together. Suddenly the horse came to an abrupt halt, their way barred by a mule. A man had been leading it and now it was standing as still as a rock, refusing to budge. The cattle pens and the crowd were so close that there was no way past. Prudence watched for a few seconds, then, as the hold-up looked as if it might last some time, she took the opportunity to clamber down.

'I'll make enquiries and see if I can find Master Mileham's house,' she called.

Since Edward was not likely to agree, she slipped away into the crowd without waiting for his reply. She bought some apples from one of the stall-holders and asked the lady if she knew where Ebenezer Mileham lived. The merchant was obviously well known, a man of substance in the neighbourhood, and his spacious house, built of beautifully knapped flint, was only a short distance from where she stood. She glanced back towards Edward and saw that the road was still blocked, and he could only sit there, quite unable to move on. She could not help smiling at the commotion that was going on around the loudly snorting mule, whose stubborn behaviour had caused a big crowd to gather round. Peals of laughter rang out as the animal resisted every effort by its owner to make it move. It looked as if the road would be blocked for several minutes.

Impulsively she hurried across the market-place to Master Mileham's house and knocked on the door. Almost immediately it was opened, and she was surprised to find herself facing an elegantly dressed gentleman, wearing an ankle-length gown of rich black damask, trimmed with scarlet and white braid. He gazed at her with a stern expression.

'Well? What do you want, young woman?' His voice was authoritative and unfriendly.

She stared back at him unflinchingly. 'I wish to see Master Ebenezer Mileham, if that is possible.'

'Yes? And what do you want with me?'

'I am Prudence Collins; you know my father, Jacob.'

He looked at her more closely, then glanced behind her, obviously surprised that she was alone. 'Your father is not with you?'

'Alas, my father is dead. We were on our way to emigrate when we were attacked by outlaws. I would have been killed also, but that gentleman sprang to my aid.'

She indicated Edward, whose head was clearly visible above the crowd as he sat on the wagon. At that precise moment someone gave the mule a mighty whack on its rump, making it rear up and toss its head so violently that its halter snapped. Freed, it snorted in delight, spun round and set off at a gallop.

The crowd parted to make way for the frenzied animal and Edward was able to move on again. She saw him turn, knew he was searching the crowd for a sight of her and waved her hand. He saw it, and even at that distance she read the look of displeasure that brought a frown to his face. She turned back to Master Mileham and saw that he was staring hard at Edward—standing immobile—almost as if he had seen a ghost. A shiver of apprehension ran chillingly down her spine.

'I cannot stop,' Prudence said hastily; somehow it seemed imperative that she should rejoin Edward on the wagon without wasting any more time. 'I merely called to ask if you had seen the families who are emigrating.'

'They were here a day or so ago. But you must step inside.'

'No—really. We have to hurry to meet up with the ship——'

'But you have ample time, Mistress Collins. It is not due to sail for a week at the earliest.'

She could scarcely believe it. 'I—I thought——'

'I insist.' To emphasis his words he reached out and grasped Prudence's arm and pulled her towards the door.

She was so surprised that she found herself almost dragged through the doorway before she realised what was happening.

'I must speak to Master Hayward,' she said.

'Master Hayward, eh?' Could it have been a sneer in Master Mileham's voice as he repeated the name? It did nothing to calm the fear that had begun to grip her. 'Don't worry about that gentleman,' he added. 'I'll send for him immediately.'

This time there was no doubt that his voice contained a threat. Prudence tried to pull away from his hold, but his grip was far too firm. She was horrified when Master Mileham beckoned to a small group of Roundhead soldiers mingling with the crowd. They came over at once—obviously Master Mileham was a man of authority in the neighbourhood.

'That man on the wagon over there is Sir Edward Benningham. Arrest him.'

Expressions of amazement, excitement and triumphant joy flitted over the faces of the four troopers as they sprang into action. 'Arrest him' Master Mileham had instructed, and the soldiers were losing no time in carrying out his order. The horror of it sank into Prudence's mind. What could she do? She must warn him; she tried to shriek 'Edward'. She opened her mouth, but before a sound could come out of it Master Mileham tugged at her arm, jerked her off balance and bundled her into the house. He slammed the heavy door shut behind her, making her a prisoner.

'Let me go. You've no right to do this to me——'

'It's for your own good, my dear child. You were quite right to come to me for protection from that vile reprobate.'

'His name is Edward Hayward...' she protested, even though she knew it was useless. She had always known that Edward was the high-ranking Cavalier officer who was hunted by Cromwell's troops, even though he had not told her. Now she cursed herself for a fool in coming to this house. Why had she not stayed with Edward, as he had wished her to?

Master Mileham pushed her through another door and into a large reception-room; its elegance was a salute to his wealth, with its walls magnificently clothed in linenfold panelling. A long table of solid oak stood in the middle, and several chairs were set around the walls.

'I cannot stay here——' she protested.

'Don't be alarmed, my dear. You'll come to no harm.' He pulled a tasselled bell-rope. 'I'll call my wife to give you refreshment——'

'I don't want refreshment—I wish to leave immediately.'

'Don't be so foolish, Prudence. This man you call Master Hayward is vile, one of the most evil of our enemies. The troops under his command looted every village they passed, ravished all the women and girls——'

He broke off as Mistress Mileham came into the room. She was tall, thin and severe of dress, although the materials of which it was made were expensive and the blackwork embroidery intricate. She was thin-lipped and hard of face, and her expression was in no way lightened as her husband introduced Prudence and explained the circumstances which had brought her there.

A commotion outside the door interrupted him, and in marched the Roundhead troopers, with Edward in their midst. His hands were tied behind his back so that he was helpless to resist their callous shoving and thumping. He glared around the room and when his eyes fell on her the expression in their dark depths held such accusation and abomination that she recoiled.

'Ah, you got him!' exclaimed Master Mileham. His voice purred maliciously, and he rubbed his hands with sadistic glee. 'What a lucky chance!' Then he turned towards her, beaming his congratulations. 'Oh, Mistress Collins, you did well to call on me for I dread to think what would have happened to you—and to countless other innocent young maidens—if this evil creature had remained at large.'

Prudence had never in her life felt so helpless. There was absolutely nothing she could say or do. Master Mileham and the soldiers knew Edward's identity, and most of Cromwell's army had been engaged in searching for him. She longed to rush to Edward, to tell him that she had never dreamed that anything like this would happen—that she had not betrayed him—but that would have been useless. The troopers had an iron grip on him, and if she displayed too much sympathy they might even arrest her too. Then there would be no chance at all of helping him. She turned away in despair— yet at the back of her active mind was the hope that perhaps she might be able to do something—find some way to rescue him.

'Take him to the town gaol,' Master Mileham instructed. 'I'll send a messenger to the Intendent, so that he can arrange the trial and execution, as soon as possible.'

Prudence could not restrain a gasp. Mistress Mileham eyed her coldly. 'Save your sympathy for those he and his men have raped and plundered,' she said. 'Hanging is too easy a punishment for such a man.'

'But you are judging him even before he has been tried,' she cried. She could scarcely believe they were talking about the same man. 'He saved me when I was in the gravest danger——' Her protestations were waved aside.

'Only because he knew you could be useful to him.' Mistress Mileham's face was puffed and reddened with rage. 'You've been a fool not to see that. Travelling with you gave him the perfect disguise. He would have been caught days ago but for that.'

That was probably true, and she had known it all along, but it had also kept her safe. She realised

that it was useless for her to plead for clemency.
She could do nothing but look on as the Roundhead
soldiers grasped the helpless Edward by his arms,
preparing to march him away.

'One moment,' Edward demanded in such a
commanding voice that the soldiers hesitated.

All eyes in the room were focused upon him, and
Prudence started forward, somehow convinced that
he wished to speak to her. He did, but when his
eyes looked directly into hers she quailed at the
contempt and repugnance she read in them. She
could only stand stock-still with her hands spread
out in an unconscious gesture of helplessness.

His lip curled. 'You couldn't wait to denounce
me, could you? I should have known better than
to trust one of your ilk.'

'Oh, Edward——' She wanted to refute the angry
accusation, to plead innocence—but could not because she was so sickeningly conscious that his
capture might never have happened if she had not
contacted the Milehams. It was she who had
brought him to this.

He interrupted harshly, 'I want to hear no lying
excuses. I can accept my fate, as an officer and a
gentleman should.' He lifted his head, every inch
the proud Cavalier, and his voice cut her like ice as
he added, 'You will find the wagon in the yard of
the inn. I wish you joy on your journey.'

'Take him away,' snapped Master Mileham.

Brutally the soldiers jerked Edward round and
gave him a vicious shove between the shoulder-
blades that sent him staggering forward. He righted
himself and marched proudly from the room. To

Prudence it felt as if her heart had been torn out and was trying of its own volition to follow him. One of the troopers closed the door, and she was gripped by a terrible fear that she would never see him again.

CHAPTER SIX

'YOU'VE done a good work today, husband,'
Mistress Mileham smirked. 'This will increase your
standing with the good Master Cromwell.'

'I dare say it will,' replied Master Mileham,
rubbing his hands together and almost crowing with
delight. 'Yes. This capture will be the talk of the
town, and will certainly do me no harm—no harm
at all.'

He spoke with smug satisfaction, and nodded at
his wife with an expression of such vicious elation
that Prudence felt her blood boiling to the point
where she longed to claw at his self-righteous face
with her bare hands.

'How fortunate that you came to me, Mistress
Collins, so that I could rid you of the company of
that rogue.' Master Mileham turned to Prudence,
nodding his head to emphasise his words.

'Even if all you say is true, Master Mileham, I
must tell you again that but for that man I would
not be alive today. He sprang to my defence after
the robbers had shot my father——'

'Probably they were all in it together—had it all
planned——'

'No,' she interrupted. 'That couldn't be. He shot
one of the outlaws.'

'An accident, no doubt.'

'Master Mileham, I beg you as a Christian to show mercy——'

'I have a duty to protect the community from men such as he. I shall do what I know to be right, and I am absolutely clear in my mind where my duty lies. Let me tell you, if you had not been useful to him you would not have remained inviolate. But you can put all that behind you now. I'll see to your safety.'

'Please——' Prudence made one last effort to make him understand, but he was no longer listening to her and continued with his plans.

'I'll arrange for an escort of troops to take you on to Harwich tomorrow. We'll look after you, won't we, my dear?' He turned to his wife. 'I'm sure we have a spare bed where Mistress Collins can stay for the night, haven't we?'

'There may be space in the attic——' Mistress Mileham's attitude was far from welcoming '—but think of your daughters, husband.'

'Please do not trouble,' Prudence said quickly. She had already decided that she could not bear to remain a moment longer in this household where there was so much dogmatic intolerance. 'My wagon and goods are all at the inn, and I shall go there too.'

Master Mileham moved towards his wife as if he would remonstrate with her, but Prudence wanted no charity. She understood exactly what Mistress Mileham was thinking—that Jacob Collins, being dead, was no longer a useful and well-to-do business contact, and therefore there was no actual necessity for her to provide hospitality to his troublesome daughter. Moreover, the fanatically narrow-minded woman felt that Prudence's character had been tainted by her close contact with Edward.

Prudence lifted her head proudly, and with a slight curl of her lip repeated, 'I shall go to the inn. On no account would I wish your daughters' reputations to be besmirched by my company.'

The hardly concealed relief that crossed Mistress Mileham's face confirmed that she had read the situation correctly, although she hid it quickly under a pretence of being affronted.

'Well, I'm sure! I don't see that you're in any position to act as if our attic is not good enough for you. Staying at the inn unaccompanied will certainly lower your reputation.'

'Only to those whose opinion I do not value,' Prudence replied coldly, and walked with swift determination across the room. Mistress Mileham huffed and her husband puffed and they both stared at her as if she had taken leave of her senses, but neither of them made any move to stop her.

That proved that they were glad to be rid of her, thought Prudence as she hurried out of the house and walked swiftly along the street through the bustling throng, making her way towards the inn. As she went she noticed a square tower with a heavy door studded with iron bolts; undoubtedly it was the gaol. On top was a large bell, which could be rung to alert the townspeople of danger—of fire, or escaping prisoners. Deliberately she made her way around it and studied the building carefully from all angles. On two sides it abutted houses; at the rear it had only a solid wall, and her heart sank as she realised there was not a single window on the ground floor.

It wrung her heart to imagine Edward locked inside there; tears pricked behind her eyes but she dashed them impatiently away—this was no time to be weak. If only she could get him out! There must be something she could do—but what? She would give anything—everything—to be able to free him. Perhaps the guards could be bribed...her box, which contained those gold coins, was on the wagon—and that was in the yard of the inn, unguarded—all her possessions were in it. A moment ago she would not have cared what happened to them; now suddenly their importance became paramount.

The belt with the key and a few coins was buckled around her waist. She picked up her skirts, hurried on as fast as she could and was soon in the cobbled yard behind the long, rambling timber-framed building of the hostelry. She breathed a sigh of relief as she saw the wagon standing alongside a wall. The horse had been taken from the shafts, and when she called out a whinny from one of the row of stables answered her. She looked in and saw that Darkie was comfortably housed and munching at some oats.

Satisfied on that score, Prudence turned to the wagon. It seemed to be just as she had left it. She lifted the blanket, looked under the seat, and saw with relief that her box was intact. Replacing the blanket with care, she crossed the yard and entered the inn. The landlord, red of face and rotund of belly, was sitting in his parlour, gossiping idly with three elderly men. He stood up as she approached and seemed to look at her so suspiciously that she feared he would be unfriendly.

'I wish to rent a room for the night, if you please,' she said in a crisp businesslike voice.

'Oh, ah!' In leisurely fashion he moved towards her, until he was out of earshot of the other men, then said in a low voice, 'Are you the young lady as the wagon belongs to?'

'I am, and I thank you for taking care of it for me.'

'I was told you would be staying with the Milehams.'

'Then you were told wrongly,' Prudence said sharply, feeling that it was no business of his. 'I wish to stay here, if that is possible.'

He leaned across and dropped his voice to a whisper. 'That was Sir Edward as you was travelling with, wasn't it?'

Prudence hesitated. She was aware that the other men had fallen silent and were regarding her with open curiosity. Did they support Cromwell—or the King? What of the landlord himself? Would they all, like the Milehams, demand that Edward be hanged? Was there anything she could do to save him? She must be careful. 'I don't know what you mean.' Her voice was cool and haughty.

A smile flickered across the landlord's face—was it friendly or vindictive? She could not be sure. 'I'll show you to your room,' he said. 'This way.'

He opened a door at the side of the fireplace and ushered her ahead of him up a narrow twisting stairway. There was a small landing at the top, leading to a pleasantly large bedroom. 'It's the best we have in the house,' he said. There was a note of pride in his voice as he leaned conspiratorially towards her. 'Fit even for Sir Edward's lady.'

Her heart leapt into her mouth. She knew there was no point in denying it, but instinct warned her to remain silent.

'I knew him the moment he drove into the yard there,' the landlord continued. 'Even with his hair cropped short and in that hat! I thought it was a rare joke, that hat,' he chuckled.

Prudence pursed her lips, remembering that the hat had been her father's though she could see how incongruous it would look to someone who really knew Edward. Could she trust this bluff, burly man who seemed to be friendly? She waited until his mirth died away and he continued.

'He couldn't fool me. He's been a-comin' in here since he was a boy, an' allus called me by my full name, Christopher Buller. Not just Kit, like most people. Used to come in here with his father, Sir Richard. An' since he's been a man he's spent many a night here.'

Was his friendship genuine? You could never tell. Prudence remained cautious, and was reluctant to be drawn into any admission she might regret later. 'This room will do perfectly well,' she said in her most matter-of-fact tone. 'Perhaps someone will help me up with my box and a few other things.'

'Certainly, my lady.'

'I'll come down and sort out what I need. And my name is Mistress Collins,' she told him firmly.

'Just as you wish, Mistress. In my trade I have to serve everyone who comes, no matter what their station in life.'

Prudence felt that she had lowered herself in his estimation by her rejection of the title 'my lady'. She was surprised to find that she did not actually dislike the designation as much as she should have. But she had no time to waste in thinking about that. She followed the landlord downstairs.

He opened the back door and called out, 'Tim, come 'ere.' Tim popped his head out of the stable, a ginger-haired lad with an impudent grin. 'Go with Mistress Collins and carry up her luggage.'

As soon as she had the box safely up in her room, and the door had closed behind the boy, Prudence unlocked it and lifted out the little bag of gold. It seemed to be intact. She tipped a few coins into her palm, dropped them into a smaller drawstring bag, then tied that to the money-belt that fitted under the waistband of her skirt, so that it hung among her petticoats, out of sight. Carefully she locked the box again and pushed it under the bed. Without waiting a moment more, she set out to visit the gaol.

An iron bell-pull hung beside the door, and in answer to her summons the heavy door creaked open. A surly-looking fellow stood and stared at her impudently, and Prudence felt her courage slip a little. 'What do you want?' he asked gruffly.

'I want to tell that black-hearted villain you've got prisoner just what I think of him,' she said, using a rough voice and sounding angry. She had decided in advance that such an attitude would be the most likely to meet with favour from the gaolers. Now that she was actually playing the unfamiliar part she felt distinctly nervous.

'Why? What's he done to you, my beauty?' The man's curiosity had been titillated.

'Never you mind.' She forced herself to look at him boldly.

The gaoler chuckled. His eyes raked appreciatively over her. 'You don't need to tell me—I can guess. Especially knowing who he is.'

'Well—are you going to let me see him?'

'I suppose it won't do no 'arm.' He opened the door and, with a toss of her head that she hoped was provocative, Prudence entered.

She found herself in a small square room, facing two other Roundhead guards who sat at a table. She was surprised to find they had been playing cards, for such frivolity was frowned upon by their Puritan leaders. Perhaps it meant they were not too rigid in their allegiance, and that might be helpful to her. What little light there was came from the small barred window in the door and a single candle.

It was a few moments before her eyes adjusted to the gloom, then she was able to make out a barred cell at the back, and a figure which must be Edward, sitting on a hard wooden bench, with his chin resting on his hands. It was an attitude of despondency, and her heart went out to him. She longed to reach out her hands to comfort him— but that would kill any chance she had of helping him to escape. She concentrated her gaze on the gaolers.

'Good day to you.'

From the corner of her eye she saw Edward's head jerk up as he recognised her voice, but still her smile was turned towards the other men.

One of the guards leapt to his feet. 'You're the young woman what was travelling with the prisoner,' he accused.

'Aye, to my sorrow. I had to go with him.' It wasn't difficult to make her voice break as if in distress. 'I was entirely in his power until we got to this town.'

'Sit down, my dear. Tell us what he did to you,' said one of the guards, with a dirty grin.

'I—I couldn't bear to,' she replied quickly.

'Like that, was it? Want me to beat him up for you?'

'No.' She said it too quickly and added, 'He'll get what's coming to him soon enough.'

She moved across to the barred doorway of the cell, and stood looking in. Edward got up as she approached and glared at her. The disappointment and anger in his face hurt her more deeply than she would have believed possible. He blamed her for his arrest, and guiltily she had to admit that it would not have happened if she had heeded his instructions not to contact the Milehams. How she wished she could get some message to him! If only she could tell him that she would do something to help, even though as yet she was not sure just what it would be.

'Come to gloat, have you?' The snarl in his voice added to the pain she felt, but with a tremendous effort she hid her feelings. She had to remember the gaolers behind her, avidly listening and watching.

'And why not?' she asked in a bright, hard voice. 'Don't expect any sympathy from me.'

He made no reply but folded his arms and stood staring at her with his lips locked tight in an angry line. Meanwhile her eyes ranged over the cell, imprinting it on her mind for future use. It was strongly barred and the door had a heavy lock; the only exit would be through the guard-room immediately in front of it. There would be no possibility of getting Edward out while the soldiers were there. Could they be bribed? Or drugged?

Deliberately she turned her back on Edward and sat down at the table. To have been able to see his face would have been an intolerable distraction, and she would have found it difficult, if not impossible, to act uncaringly, as she knew she must. Then with all the charm she could muster, which was by no means inconsiderable, she set about engaging the three gaolers in conversation.

The company of an entertaining young woman made a welcome break from boredom, and the men vied with each other to catch her attention. As they chatted, her mind was busy, sorting out the measure of each one of them as an individual. She decided that the ginger-haired one called Nat might be the most likely to help her. He was an unhappy young man, not long married, who longed to go home. He hated being in the army.

'Where is your home, Nat?' she asked.

'Not far from 'ere. Just outside Harwich—wish I was there now.'

Prudence nodded sympathetically, but inwardly she was cherishing this piece of information. There might be a way she could use it to her advantage. She must speak to Nat alone.

'Thirsty work, sittin' about here,' she said, presently. 'I'm lodgin' at the inn. Fancy a jug of beer?'

'Not 'alf.'

'Long as you don't give none of it to 'im.' She tossed her head in Edward's direction. It gave her an opportunity to look at him, as she constantly longed to do. He was lying on the hard bench at the back of the cell, with his back to her. He appeared to be sleeping, but somehow she knew that he was actually wide awake.

'That'd be a waste of good ale,' agreed the gaoler.

Prudence stood up. 'A big jug'll be heavy. How about you comin' wi' me, Nat?'

He leapt to his feet and opened the outer door for her. It had not been locked, simply held on a strong iron latch. Prudence kept up the conversation as they walked together to the inn, asking him about his wife, who was expecting her first baby in only a few weeks' time.

'Let me have a look on my wagon—see if there's anything I can send her as a present. I can't let you have any of the bedding—I'll need that for the voyage—but how about this lace cap? I made it myself.'

'It's very pretty. Mary would be greatly charmed with that.'

'There you are, then. How long is it since you've seen her?'

'Too long,' Nat grumbled. 'Must be five or six months. I been away fighting all that time, when I should've been at home looking after the land. My father died last year. Mary and my mother have done their best, but its been hard for them without a man.'

'You'll get home soon, I reckon,' said Prudence.

'I've been told to wait for my pay, otherwise I'd be off tomorrow, whether they give me leave or not. War's over, I reckon. The King's a prisoner; ain't nothing more to fight for.'

He might help her if she made it worth his while, but she dared not risk asking too soon. 'Come on— let's get that jug of ale,' she said.

Prudence encouraged the gaolers to drink as much as they wished, and as the time passed and the strong brew loosened their tongues they grumbled freely about the conditions under which they served. Nat was the one who drank least. He was a simple, hard-working young man, abstemious by nature.

'May as well drink and be merry while we may,' said one. 'The Intendent'll be here tomorrow morning early, an' they're goin' ter 'ave the trial straight away. They're putting up the gallows ready.'

Prudence shivered. While the talk had flowed around her, her mind had been busy. That appalling information made it imperative that she wasted no more time. 'I'll buy you some more beer,' she offered. 'Come and help me, Nat.'

As soon as they were alone together she grasped his arm and turned him to face her so that she could look directly into his eyes. 'Nat—what would you

say if I asked you to drive my horse and wagon to
Harwich for me?'

His eyes glowed at the thought, and she saw that
he was tempted. 'I could go home——' That was
his immediate reaction, then his eyes narrowed and
he looked at her with a trace of suspicion. 'You
mean—go along wi' you?'

'Not exactly. I'm thinking of riding there on
horseback.'

'Alone?'

'No,' she admitted slowly, unwilling to reveal too
much of her plan to him. 'I expect to have a companion. But that need not concern you. All you
have to do is to drive my wagon to the dock at
Harwich. I should be there before you; if not you
must wait until I arrive.' Her voice revealed none
of the doubts she felt. She was well aware of the
danger that lay ahead—if she was caught assisting
a prisoner to escape it would be death for her as
well as for Edward. She refused to think of it.
Steadily she continued with her instructions. 'When
I join you I'll remove my goods, but I'll have no
more need of the horse and wagon and I'll give
them to you in thanks for your services.'

She was placing great trust in him. He might
simply take all her goods and never be seen again,
but she judged him to be an honest young man. It
was a risk she had to take, for she would never be
able to get Edward out of gaol on her own. Nat
regarded her steadily and she waited, forcing herself
to be patient. He was not a quick thinker. She could
almost read his thoughts as, one after the other,
expressions crossed his open countenance, re-

vealing surprise, doubt, hope and disbelief. Desperately she prayed he would not ask too many questions.

His eyes narrowed. 'I'd have to see this horse and wagon,' he said.

Evidently he was weighing up the value of the horse and wagon against the risk he would run.

'It's a sturdy little wagon, Nat. Not new, but in good condition. As for the horse, I reckon he's got ten years work in him yet.'

'Oh, ah.' Nat resumed his contemplative attitude. He would be absent without leave, but that happened often enough; he was of little consequence in the army's view, and he might scarcely be missed. It was too good an offer to refuse.

'All you want is for me to drive the wagon to the docks and wait there for you?'

'That's all.'

'Then I can take the horse and wagon, and it'll belong to me?'

'You have my word on it. His name is Darkie.'

'That's nice,' he paused. Prudence held her breath. 'When do you want me to set out?'

She exhaled a sigh of relief. 'Later tonight.'

He shook his head. 'Wouldn't be safe to travel at night.'

'It has to be tonight, Nat. If you wait till the morning it'll be too late.'

'Tell you what I could do—I got a cousin who lives about four miles down the road. I wouldn't mind goin' that far in the dark. I could stay with him overnight.'

'You'd get on the road before dawn tomorrow?' she asked anxiously. 'There's no time to be wasted—besides, you'd get home that much earlier.'

'The sooner the better, as far as I'm concerned.'

'Good. That's settled. Now there are just one or two other things I need your help with.'

He drew back and his eyes narrowed suspiciously. 'What things?'

'Do you think you can get a quiet word to the landlord?'

'Kit Buller? Course I can.'

'Tell him I'd like to speak with him out here. You can leave the jug with me.'

Nat handed it over, and set off on his errand. Prudence hurried to the little wagon, lifted the tilt and found the small box in which she kept herbs and medicaments. She knew exactly what she sought and it was the work of a moment to tip a small phial of powder into the jug. By the time Nat came back with the landlord she had straightened the covers and was moving towards the inn.

'Get the jug filled, Nat, and take it to your companions at the gaol,' she instructed, handing it to him, together with some small coins. Then she lowered her voice to a whisper and added, 'Don't drink any of it yourself. I want you sober when you drive my horse and wagon. I'll join you at the gaol very soon.'

'Aye.' Nat darted away. If he did not heed her warning, and drank from that jug, her whole plan would be wrecked, but all she could do was to carry on hopefully.

She turned towards the landlord with a smile intended to hide the tension she felt. 'Thank you for coming out, Master Buller. I wished to ask if you have two good riding horses I can hire.'

'Two?' he queried, sounding surprised.

'Two, and the best you have,' she confirmed steadily. 'I want them saddled and ready in half an hour.'

'It'll be getting dusk by then,' he objected. 'Not a good time for travelling. Outlaws, you know— footpads...highwaymen...'

Prudence shivered. 'I'll pay you well.'

'You'll need to. Goin' to 'arwich, is it?'

'To board ship,' she told him sharply. 'I'm joining a group of friends bound for America.'

'What about your wagon?'

'I've made arrangements. I'll pay you now for stabling the horse and the hire of the room.' She was growing a little weary of his endless questions and her voice was sharp. 'Have you got horses to hire, or not?'

'I have. As good as you'll get anywhere in the county.' He lowered his voice and leaned towards her. 'Good enough for Sir Edward an' his lady, I reckon.'

His words took her by surprise; her instinct was to deny it, but she knew that would have been useless. She felt shaken—and very vulnerable. Was the esteem in which Christopher Buller had held Sir Richard and, she hoped, Edward also high enough for him to remain silent? One word from the landlord to Master Mileham and, far from helping

Edward to escape, Prudence would join him inside the prison cell. She must not think on those lines.

'Bring out these horses you say are so fine,' she ordered.

'You won't be disappointed.'

Soon an ostler, helped by Tim, was parading a magnificent pair of animals before her. She could have asked for no better.

'They'll do,' she said, thankful for that little bag of gold coins. 'Name your price.' It was no time for quibbling.

Master Buller did not answer her immediately, but turned to his ostler. 'Get them saddled and ready.' Only when they were alone did he state a figure—as she had expected, it was quite high. She agreed it with a brusque nod of her head.

'Where was you aimin' to pick up your—er—fellow traveller?' Master Buller asked.

He knew. There was no doubt about it. Still she hesitated, playing a sort of cat-and-mouse game with him. 'I'll tell you that later.'

'I'll bring 'em out myself. Take 'em for a little canter into the woods, like somewhere up behind the gaol?'

That would be an ideal arrangement, if only she could be sure she could trust him! Suppose he was setting up a trap? Catching a malefactor on the run would bring him a rich reward—and, as Prudence would then be an offender too, he could help himself to her goods. Perhaps he even knew about the gold coins in her box under the bed. But she had no alternative. She was in no position to refuse help. If she did nothing Edward would be tried in the morning and almost certainly hanged the following day.

'Would you do that?' she asked, looking earnestly into Christopher Buller's face.

He turned away. Was he unwilling to meet her eyes? 'You give me the money and I'll be there.'

'I'll need saddlebags,' she remembered.

'Of course,' he agreed. 'And the money? When will I get the money?'

'I'll meet you in the parlour with it.'

He nodded and moved towards the stable. Prudence hurried into the inn, up to her room, dropped to her knees and reached under the bed. She pulled out the box and unlocked it. Everything was intact. She counted out the coins to pay the landlord, then scooped the rest into the drawstring bag. She took letters and documents in their leather folder, and rolled up a few personal items in a linen square. Everything else she would have to trust to Nat with the wagon. She called for the houseboy to carry her box down and saw it safely stowed under the passenger seat as before. She returned to the inn and paid the landlord, then she walked along towards the gaol.

Her instinct was to hurry, but she forced herself to keep a normal pace, wishing to attract as little attention as possible. She knocked lightly on the door. Her heart was thumping madly as she wondered what she would find inside. Without waiting for a reply, she lifted the latch and stepped through. Nat stood facing her, his ginger hair tousled and a wide grin spread over his freckled face. The other two gaolers were sprawled from the bench and over the table, out to the world. Prudence had scarcely dared to hope that her potion would have been so effective.

Edward was standing behind the iron grille that made a door to the cell. His eyes met hers, watching her closely, without a flicker of warmth, his handsome face contorted by an almost savage expression that seemed to be directed at her. It was as if nothing that was happening in the room was in any way connected with him, making him icily remote, and her heart contracted with inexplicable pain. She had no time to question; she thrust the feeling aside, sure that she could put it right later. Just now there was too much to do; danger was all around and lying ahead. Time was pressing. At any moment her plan might go horribly and hopelessly wrong. She closed the door behind her.

'The keys,' she demanded of Nat.

He grabbed the hair of one of the guards and jerked his head off the table, revealing the bunch of keys held together by an iron ring. He picked them up and handed them to her.

'That one will unlock the cell.'

'You'd better start off, Nat,' she said.

'Right away,' he agreed with a cheery grin. 'See you at the docks.'

The door closed behind him and Prudence ran towards the cell door. She thrust the key into the lock and, grasping it with both hands, managed to turn it. Then she flung open the door and stood smiling, triumphant, her head upturned in joyous greeting, ready to fling herself into his arms. She was convinced that Edward would now understand exactly what she was doing—but he made no move. He simply stood there, by the side of the open door, holding the iron bars of the cell. He stared down at her, and his face was set in such grim lines that she took a step back.

'What made you change your mind?' he growled.

CHAPTER SEVEN

ALMOST immediately Prudence recovered from the shock of Edward's question. Did he think she had welcomed his arrest? Such a thought was not worthy of an answer. How could he hold such a low opinion of her? She dismissed it sharply.

'Quick. I've horses waiting in the woods behind the gaol.' He made no move, just stared at her. She began to wonder if the guards had relented and given Edward some of the doped ale. Impatiently she grabbed his hand. 'Come on. I don't know how long before those guards wake up.'

It was as if until that moment he had not focused his mind on the fact that he was free. Then dynamically he sprang into action, hurtled himself out of the cell, and his hand closed around hers in a grip so firm that it hurt. He glanced back, wrenched the bunch of keys from the lock, dropped her hand, ran over to the guards and snatched up the horse-pistol that was lying on the table. Then he rushed towards the outer door. Prudence followed close behind him.

'Let me look out first,' she suggested.

Edward ignored her. Perhaps he still did not trust her, or perhaps his unexpected freedom had gone to his head, but he would stop for nothing at that moment. He rushed outside into the darkness. For a horrible moment she thought he would lock her inside, but he hustled her out, and together they stood, still and silent in the cool night air. It was when he turned and shut the door with quiet caution that she knew he was back to normal. The characteristic cool control she had observed in his actions previously had reasserted itself. He locked the door of the gaol, and removed the keys.

'Which way?' he demanded in a whisper, his face close to hers.

'Up behind the gaol.'

He took long strides and Prudence was taxed to the limit to keep up with him. She was panting before they reached the shelter of the trees. Then he stopped briefly. A dog barked somewhere in the distance. They both looked back down on the little town, which seemed to be sleeping peacefully. He threw the bunch of keys into some brambles; they made a clinking sound, then again all was still. Prudence was alert, tense, listening for a call or some sound that would tell her the landlord had kept his word.

'Where are these horses?' Edward asked, suspicion again adding a harsh tone to his voice.

'We'll have to walk on a bit further,' she said with more confidence than she felt. Had she been right to trust Christopher Buller?

Edward held the horse-pistol ready in his hand as they moved deeper into the wood. Prudence found the going hard and wished that he would take her hand, for the hill was quite steep and the darkness inside the wood made the walk difficult. An owl hooted as if in derision. Prudence strained her ears, and at last heard a faint whinny, a stamping of hooves.

'Master Buller?' she called softly.

'My lady?' She was immensely relieved to recognise the voice and certainly in no mood to reprove him for addressing her again by that title.

Edward sprang ahead of her and she could see the horses as she emerged from the shadow of the trees to a grassy bridleway. Her relief that the landlord had kept his promise was immeasurable. Edward recognised Christopher Buller and greeted him warmly.

'I've brought you my best horses, Sir Edward. And the saddlebags, just as your lady ordered. There's a holster for your horse-pistol.'

'Thank you, Christopher.'

'A bargain's a bargain,' he replied crisply. 'The young lady arranged it. I've done my part and now I'm off.' He handed over the reins. 'I couldn't let those bigoted fanatics hang you. I dare not stay——'

'Go, old friend. My heartfelt thanks. Don't put yourself in any more danger.'

'I'll wish you Godspeed, sir.' Christopher Buller backed away a couple of steps, then turned and set off down the hill towards the town at a shambling run as if the devil himself might be on his tail.

Fear was making them all move quickly. Prudence was close to Edward. 'Ready?' he asked, handing her the reins of the smaller of the two horses.

She put her foot into his cupped hands and he threw her up into the saddle; she held the little horse in while Edward mounted, then, without another word, at the fastest possible speed they were away. Prudence was grateful that he knew which direction to take, for she was quite lost. The brightness of the moonlight would have gilded the ride with romantic beauty, but for the constant fear of discovery and recapture.

The bridleway stretched away through the woods, then turned sharply as they came to a clearing. They scarcely slowed their mounts, but carried on, the horses' hooves thundering on the hard track, the miles passing. Edward was usually a little ahead, but Prudence kept up with grim determination. Here and there they passed a hovel or two, wood framed, infilled with daub and wattle, straw-thatched or peat-roofed. Poor dwellings where families struggled for existence, keeping a few pigs in the woods and tilling their small patch of land.

They kept up a good pace, Edward leading the way and glancing back occasionally, checking that she had not got lost, she thought with a grimace. There was silence between them, but Prudence did not find it oppressive—she was far too occupied with the problem of guiding her willing and speedy horse along while keeping a look-out for any low-hanging branches on the trees. After they had ridden for half an hour or more the track widened to become a rutted dusty lane. Ahead of them stood a high wide archway flanked by thick thorn hedges.

Edward rode through it without checking his speed and she followed, along a lane that led across a broad expanse of meadowland, where sheep grazed. Further on, the lane divided, the left fork continuing on, and the right-hand one sweeping towards a pile of blackened ruins which must have been a very fine manor house. It had evidently been destroyed by fire quite recently, reducing it to a shell of crumbling walls, roofless, with twisted chimneys of decorative brickwork which now pointed upwards, starkly useless. A black hole gaped where the grand entrance door had been; rubble and scorched timbers were strewn down the wide step and over the stone terrace. The formal garden had been trampled beneath the feet of men and horses, once-elegant statues toppled over and beheaded. Prudence gasped in horror at such desecration.

'What is this?' she asked.

'All that is left of Tillington Manor,' he answered bitterly.

Edward rode close up to the house, then reined in and sat very still and straight, his head turning this way and that as he gazed around. It reminded Prudence forcibly of what had happened to her home in Norwich—and anger at the senseless destruction welled up in her. Her heart was heavy with sympathy, for she had no doubt this once beautiful house had been the seat of the Benninghams. One glance at his tightly compressed lips and the iron control that held his face rigid confirmed her assessment. There was nothing she could say.

'Those gaolers that you were so fond of boasted that they personally set the torches to my house,' Edward said, his voice icy with controlled fury and despair.

Prudence gasped. It did not surprise her that the gaolers had been responsible for this arson. She judged them capable of almost anything, but she was deeply hurt at the implied criticism of her relationship with the gaolers. Surely he must realise why she had acted as she did?

'I had no fondness for them,' she said sharply.

'That was not how I saw it—and no one had a better view.'

'How else could I have gained entrance——?'

'You did not hear how they spoke of you when you were not there. I will not repeat the names they used—and with justification.'

An angry flush suffused her cheeks, but she tried to keep calm. 'Whatever they said, it was not my fault.'

'It was the way you had led them to think of you.'

'They wouldn't have allowed me into the gaol otherwise. Oh, Edward, surely you could see——?'

'I saw and heard everything. It was an excellent performance.'

'But that's all it was. An act—to get you out.'

'The way you played your part showed that you weren't the innocent maiden you've been leading me to believe.' His voice was icy, and it cut into her heart.

'I've helped you to escape—aren't you glad?'

'Oh, yes. I am indeed. But don't expect me to thank you, since it was you who brought about my arrest by deliberately going to that bigoted friend of yours after I warned you not to.'

'I didn't understand. I was horrified, and I felt so guilty. I had to do something...' She hesitated to pour out her feelings, to say 'I couldn't bear to think what would happen to you', for that would show how much she cared for him, and he would only pour scorn on her. Instead she said, 'It was the least I could do, after you saved me from the outlaws.'

'Aye, that's more like the truth of the matter. I accept you have a conscience—and I also know you lack the courage to travel on alone. You find me useful as an escort—I dare say you would rather trust your safety to me than to that scoundrel Nat.'

'Nat is all right. I believe he's honest. I've sent him on ahead with the wagon.'

'Have you, indeed? Then you are even more gullible than I thought. You didn't see him as I did. He taunted me more than the other two. You can wave goodbye to your wagon and everything on it.'

The safety of the wagon and its contents seemed the least of her worries at that moment. 'I pray you are wrong. But there's nothing I can do about that now.'

'Aye, we shall see—if we ever reach Harwich.'

It was useless to argue with him. She tried to soothe him. 'I understand how you must be suffering when you see your lovely home like this——'

'It is not mine,' he interrupted harshly. 'Your friend Noll Cromwell sequestered the whole estate. Not a single blade of grass belongs to me. I have no right here—and I have no wish ever to stand on this spot again. Let's go. We've wasted too much time as it is.'

He swung his horse round and set the animal off at a gallop, and Prudence immediately followed.

His cruel words, his false assessment of her action stung her to such fury that she set her mount going at top speed. One effect of the day she had spent plotting, scheming and worrying about him had been to make her realise that in some strange way she had come to care for him. She had begun to feel warmth—friendship—towards him. Of course, it couldn't be love—there was no question of that— but the days they had travelled together had induced a close companionship such as she had never felt towards any man before.

It wasn't always a comfortable feeling—often she had felt threatened by him, and upset. His actions and words ruffled and disquieted her. His virile masculinity was a danger—she knew that and had been on her guard against it. She was glad she had been able to stand out so strongly when he had kissed her, and she vowed she would never let that happen again. And yet—the touch of his lips on her had been so seductively exciting that she felt a weakness in the pit of her stomach just remembering it. There was a great deal in him that she admired, even though they were totally opposed in their main beliefs and loyalties. It distressed her more than she would have believed possible that he had formed such an ill opinion of her—she wished they could have been friends. In spite of all she had done, the atmosphere between them was more strained than ever.

He was galloping away along the moonlit grassy lane as if the devil himself was on his tail. She urged her horse on, determined to catch up with him, but the faster she rode, the faster he went, keeping always several lengths ahead of her. He had no thought of her—that was obvious. Only when Edward passed beyond the bounds of the land that had belonged to him did he slow down.

By that time a brooding resentment had begun to take hold of Prudence. Why should she care what he thought of her? She had risked everything to free him—and she had succeeded. He had saved her life and now she had returned the favour. In a few hours' time they would be at Harwich, and she would be in the company of people of her own sort, men and women whose views she understood. Then their ways would part and Edward would be off— where to she had no idea and, she told herself firmly, she certainly did not care.

Now, when she could easily have caught up with him, she deliberately rode a couple of lengths behind. Soon it would be dawn. If the escape had not yet been discovered it very soon would be. The same thought must have occurred to Edward, for he stopped and waited for her. They were on the edge of the wood, on a slightly raised piece of ground which sloped down to a ribbon of grey dust.

'The road to Harwich,' he said. His voice held a note of thoughtful satisfaction.

Her heart lifted with a flash of relief, then almost immediately steadied. 'How much further?' she questioned anxiously.

'Fifteen—perhaps eighteen miles.'

She digested that information. It meant another day's travelling. They sat side by side, not speaking, and she waited patiently, allowing him to take the decision of what they should do next. The silence was broken by the sound of horses' hooves on the road. It set a prickling of fear racing down Prudence's spine. Instinctively she backed her horse a little, prayed that the animals would keep silent.

It seemed an age before the horsemen came into view, a troop of Cromwellian cavalry, armed with swords and horse-pistols, wearing breastplates and lobster-pot helmets. The horses plodded along, and the men were weary-looking as if they had been in the saddle all night—they did not bother even to glance around. She watched until they had moved on down the long road and around a bend. The sight of them made Prudence realise just how tired she was. They passed beyond her line of vision, and she breathed a sigh of relief. Until then she had been too keyed up, with every sense so taut that she had not had time to think about anything other than keeping going. Now she felt her body sagging and became aware of an uncomfortable ache in her arms and legs. She glanced towards Edward and saw that he was dismounting. He came round to the head of her horse and held it.

'We'd better lie low during the day and travel on again after dark.' He spoke in a low voice.

She slipped down from her saddle. Her knees, reacting to the strain of riding so far and so hard, felt as if they would give way under her. She steadied herself by holding on to the stirrup leather, ashamed of her weakness. She waited for some lead from Edward. He was looking around, but she could see nothing except for trees—no shelter, nothing in which they might be hidden.

'We'll walk back a little way,' Edward decided. 'I noticed a hut.'

Prudence nodded. She followed silently. She did not recollect the hut. She was tired and her mind had been on other things. He clearly knew where he was going. When they reached it the hut was nothing but a one-roomed shack, built in log-cabin style, and so tucked away among the trees that it almost merged with them. The broken-hinged door stood ajar, and Edward looked inside.

'Not much comfort, I fear,' he commented. 'But it's dry and looks reasonably clean.'

'As long as it's safe,' Prudence said. She was beginning to feel that her legs would not carry her a step further.

'You have a sleep and I'll keep guard.' It sounded like an order.

'What about you?' she asked.

'I'll be all right, I'm used to going without sleep. Besides, I was resting yesterday in the gaol, while you were racing around with your friend Nat.'

She shook her head sadly; she was too tired even to defend herself. 'If that's what you think,' she shrugged dispiritedly.

She was glad he made no further comment on that matter. He said, 'Hand me your reins; I'll find somewhere to rest and water the horses.'

She almost staggered into the hut, and, holding on to the door-jamb, glanced briefly around. There was nothing inside, no window, no fireplace. A sweetly fragrant smell of herbs hung in the air and puzzled her, but the light was too dim for her to see where the perfume came from. It was pleasant and soothing and she was too weary to bother. It must be a woodman's shelter, and perhaps he was something of a herbalist too. It was a little disturbing to realise that the hut had been used recently, but Edward had said he would keep guard, and that knowledge calmed her anxiety. At one side the floor was strewn with bracken, quite fresh and clean. She lay down on it and slept.

The sun was high in the sky and filtering through the trees when she awoke. It was a moment before she remembered where she was. Then realisation dawned and instinctively she lay still, turning only her head, and immediately her eyes rested on the masculine bulk that was Edward. He was sitting quite close beside her. He had said he would keep guard and she could see from the upright line of his powerful body that he was indeed alert. The horse-pistol he had taken from the guard lay beside him. His face was in profile, and quite unexpectedly a stirring of emotional excitement swept over her. She could not tear her eyes away from the handsome, chiselled outline of his strong forehead, shapely nose and that wide, disturbingly sensual mouth.

He was sitting on the ground, so close that her Puritan upbringing told her it was most improper. It was even worse that she was lying there on the bed of bracken, just looking at his features and finding joy in the very sight of them. She must make him move away at once, she decided. She had to defend her modesty, and opened her mouth ready to tell him in no uncertain terms just how indecorously she thought he was behaving.

She had assumed he did not realise she was awake, but before the words of censure that had sprung into her mind could be voiced his hand had shot out from his side and caught hold of hers in that iron, bone-crushing grip she had felt more than once before. The gasp of pain that almost burst from her was stifled as she realised he was warning her of danger. He turned towards her, tapping his lips with one long, sinewy finger. She had realised his body was tight-sprung, ready for action; now she saw the tension in his face. All the perils of the previous night flooded back into her consciousness. Her heart thudded painfully. She dared not ask and strained her ears for some sound that might give her a clue what—or who—it was that now menaced them. She heard only the soughing of the wind in the branches.

Silently Edward rose to his feet; even in his jackboots he managed to pad softly to a position where he could look further out through the open door while still keeping himself hidden. A couple of minutes ticked by and then she heard voices— female voices. At least two women were coming in their direction. The aromatic bouquet of drying plants wafted all around her again, warm and heady, and, now that her eyes were adjusted to the dimness and it was full daylight, she was able to make out bunches of meadowsweet, corn mint, woodruff and tansy hanging from the rafters. Suddenly she knew. The women were herbalists, or—

she drew in a deep breath at the terrible thought—perhaps they were witches!

Panic seized her. Perhaps the women would put a spell on them. She would have scrambled to her feet and run, but Edward still held tightly to her hand, pinning her down. The women's voices were coming nearer, and something in the ill-natured tone of their voices told her they were gossiping, but she could not make out what they were saying. She felt utterly helpless; even her mind seemed to go blank—they were cornered, and she had no doubt that they would be discovered. What would happen then?

'It was that Betsy Martin. You know the one I mean...'

She lifted her head and found she could make out words—the women must be very near—then Prudence gasped as Edward flung himself towards her. In one quick movement he fell on top of her, pushing her back on to the bed of bracken, immobilising her body with the heaviness of his own. To her horror he even began to pull up her skirts, his hand reaching her bare thigh above her knitted stockings and beneath her petticoats—she prayed he would not reach higher, to her nakedness, and writhed at being unable to protest because he had covered her mouth with his own. She could scarcely breathe as he kissed her, more powerfully, more assertively even than he had done before. She tried to struggle but the weight of his body was pressing down on hers far too heavily, relentlessly. The voices were still coming nearer, the one recounting, the other eagerly expressing disapproval.

'Oh, I tell you, Martha—that Betsy Martin's a hoyden. I've got a good mind to denounce her——'

'You're right, Millicent—I've seen her myself...'

Prudence knew that Edward's actions were only a ploy, but the indecency, the sexuality of it was deeply distressing to her. He pushed open her legs, and she could do nothing but lie there helplessly. She was horrified, but had to submit, to lie beneath his heaving body, stifled by his kisses, pinned under his weight, shamed and humiliated.

The voices continued until the women must be at the door. Still they continued to chatter animatedly. 'Only this morning she was running through the fields with—— Oh!'

The woman's voice broke off with a screech. Edward lifted his head slightly, and as he did so Prudence was able to look over his shoulder, and saw clearly the shocked expressions on the faces of two plump middle-aged women. Both wore high-crowned Puritan hats, which cast shadows, but could not entirely hide the little beady eyes as round as currants, and their mouths which had dropped open in horrified surprise. One stood in the doorway and the other was craning her neck to see over her companion's shoulder. It was a moment before they recovered, a moment when time stood still, and Prudence wished with all her heart that they would turn and rush away, but they stood there as if they had been turned into stone.

'Disgraceful!' screamed the front one. 'Just look at that hoyden, sprawled out there!'

'Is it that Betsy Martin?' asked the other one eagerly.

'It's shocking. Don't look——'

'Oooh!' The woman at the back had managed to position herself where she could see better. 'Whatever is the world coming to? Who is it, Martha?'

Martha leaned forward, peering towards them. 'Betsy? Is that you, Betsy Martin?' She moved a step nearer.

Edward suddenly reached out a hand towards her, caught hold of the hem of her skirt and jerked at it. His action took her by surprise and she jumped back in alarm. With a piercing scream she turned and ran out of the hut, almost knocking Millicent over in her haste. That woman obviously had no wish to remain there alone, and immediately turned and fled after Martha.

The moment they were out of the door Edward leapt to his feet and strode across to make sure they had left. There was the snap of twigs breaking as they hurried away, with Millicent calling piteously after Martha, 'Wait for me...'

CHAPTER EIGHT

PRUDENCE hastily stood up and brushed down her disordered skirts. Never had she felt so dishevelled and embarrassed. She glared at Edward, and her anger increased as she saw his face was suffused in laughter.

'What a sight!' he chuckled. 'Did you ever come across such a couple of old busybodies?'

The answer was that she had, many a time, but she guessed that if she told him so he would merely turn it back at her with some scathing remark. How could he stand there, laughing as if he had not a care in the world? Had he forgotten that they were in imminent danger? He was acting as if his mind was deranged.

'I cannot see anything to laugh about,' she said angrily. 'I have never been so humiliated in all my life."

'Oh, come now, Prudence—was it so very terrible?'

'To me it was,' she snapped.

His smile broadened, quite patronisingly, she thought, and he held his head a little to one side. With mock seriousness he assumed an air of deep contemplation. 'I certainly could not agree with you on that point.' He shook his head and his laughter subsided. A meaningful look sprang into his dark eyes, and when he spoke again his words were uttered with slow deliberation. 'I found an element of—excitement—in my position. Perhaps it was not ecstatically so—but most definitely it was not distasteful to me.'

Her cheeks flushed hotly, and she was not sure whether it was from anger or embarrassment, her feelings were so mixed. She stamped her foot in rage, fuming because she could think of no adequate reply.

He executed an elaborate bow in her direction. 'I salute you, Betsy Martin!'

That really was the last straw! 'How dare you call me by that girl's name?' she snapped.

His merry chuckle burbled through the hut again. 'The wench sounds well worth knowing,' he said with deliberate wickedness.

'Then go and seek her out. I've no doubt you'll find her better company than me.'

He sighed. 'I wouldn't mind betting she has a greater sense of humour. She would need it to survive in the same village as those old women.'

In fury she jumped to her feet, preparing to march indignantly out of the hut. 'I'm going. I can't stay here a moment longer. The sooner I get to Harwich and in the company of decent folk, the better pleased I shall be. You may do what you wish. Just tell me where the horses are.'

His face sobered at once. 'Hush, my dear Prudence; there is no need to be so precipitate——'

'There is—there is! Don't you realise those women will be back—and they'll bring half the village with them?'

'Possibly——'

'Certainly,' she flashed back. 'We must move at once.'

'I doubt if the urgency is as great as you think,' he said laconically.

'They'll tell everyone that we were in their hut.' She almost screamed the words at him. Could she never make him understand?

He shook his head. 'They won't come looking for strangers. They'll tell everyone what Betsy Martin was up to in their hut,' he corrected. 'I fear the poor girl's name will be blackened still further— unless she has a foolproof alibi.'

She viewed the matter in that very different perspective, and was obliged to accept that he might well be right. Those women were the type that thrived on malicious gossip—suddenly she found herself feeling rather sorry for Betsy. But when Edward chuckled again and added, 'You gave a very convincing performance, my dear Prudence,' she would dearly have liked to hit him—very hard.

In a more conciliatory manner, he said, 'But, of course, you are right—it is time that we moved on.'

In a leisurely manner that increased her aggravation he sauntered over to the corner of the hut, lifted the saddles and bags, slung them over his arm, then picked up the horse-pistol. Weighty though they were, he carried all with ease, walked out of the hut and stood gazing around. She followed him.

'England is very beautiful on an afternoon like this,' he said.

The sunshine was brilliant, the trees were just beginning to show signs of approaching autumn, the ground beneath them dry, dappled with sunlight and shadows. The loveliness and peace of the woodland scene had something of a calming effect. The life cycle of nature was there all about them, with tussocks of grass, and freshly fallen leaves covering those of previous years, already decomposed into leaf-mould. Fungi thrust up through them with vigour, and burst from the stumps of trees, uprooted by gales of long ago. Now there was only a gentle breeze, which stirred high up in the green canopy above their heads.

She felt a sharp pang at the thought that she was about to leave behind so much that was familiar to her. America was new and unknown. Only a few more hours' riding and they would be at the coast. So many dangers to be faced—and there was no way now but forward. Anxiety kept her keyed up; she wanted to be moving again.

'Where did you leave the horses?' she asked.

'This way,' he said, setting off at such a smart pace that she had to lift her skirts and trot now and again to keep up with him. They had to take a zigzag path around the trees, ducking under hanging branches, and side-stepping spreading patches of nettles. She quickly lost her sense of direction and would have found it difficult to retrace their steps back to the hut. She hoped Edward knew where he was going.

'Did you bring any food?' he asked.

'Some bread and a wedge of cheese, though I'm afraid it may all be a bit stale,' she told him.

'No matter. We'll keep it for later.'

Half a furlong further and she saw the horses—
they were hobbled and grazing contentedly in a
clearing. The animals were obviously refreshed and
in good condition, and she realised that Edward
had attended to them well and had probably even
brushed them down with handfuls of dry grass. She
felt a touch of guilt that he had done that while she
had been sleeping.

He began at once to saddle up. She moved to the
other side of the horse so that she could help in the
harnessing.

'Will it be safe to travel in daylight?' she queried,
remembering why they had decided to lie low at
dawn that morning.

'We'll have to move with care, but now that
you've had a sleep it should be possible.'

'You didn't have any sleep.'

'I've rested enough, and I've thought out a way
we can take to avoid the main road to Harwich.'

'Where we saw the troops moving at dawn?'

'That would be too dangerous. We'll travel by
back ways; I recall a smuggler's track that will take
us towards the coast. It's a little further, perhaps,
but I believe it will be safer.'

They had saddled her horse and now turned to
deal with his. It surprised her that they could work
so well in unison when they were so much at
loggerheads. Reaching under the warm belly of the
patient animal, her fingers touched Edward's and
she withdrew her hand quickly, as if she had been
stung. The sensation of being pinned beneath him,
while his strong masculine body pressed hers into
her bed of bracken, remained too vivid for her peace

of mind. He had made her more sensually conscious of her own femininity then ever before. Straightening up, she met his eyes across the saddle and there was in his expression a meaning that twisted her heart and sent tingling pulses throbbing up and down the whole length of her body.

'Calm yourself, Prudence,' he said, and ridiculously those words added to her confusion. It seemed as if he understood the extraordinary feelings she was experiencing. 'You should know by now that I will do you no harm. Surely you don't need me to tell you that this afternoon's incident will not be repeated?'

What could she say? It was too awful to remember that the pressure of his body lying so intimately on top of hers had given her a shameful sensation of pleasure. She knew that she would not easily be able to forget those emotions, but never would she admit to having them.

'It most certainly will not, if I can avoid it,' she told him with perhaps a shade too much emphasis.

'Can you suggest any other ruse that would have sent those women rushing away so fast, and seeing so little?' he persisted. 'And, in its way, the incident was delightful.'

'I suppose it was—necessary,' she said grudgingly. 'I would hardly say *delightful*.'

'I fear that is a matter we will have to leave for future discussion,' he said, with a wry smile.

'I have no wish to discuss the matter ever again.'

'But I have, and I feel sure that one day we will.' He was every bit as positive as she. He tightened the last buckle of the harness, and pushed the pistol into the holster. 'Indeed, I'm quite convinced that I shall be able to change your mind on that point——'

'You'd be wasting your breath, for we have nothing in common,' she interrupted.

'I grant that it may take time,' he continued, undaunted. 'That is why we must forgo the pleasure of such an interesting conversation today.'

The horses were both ready and, wasting no more time, Edward cupped his hands, she placed one foot in them and mounted. In seconds he was also in the saddle, and they set off. Again she followed him. They did not move as fast as they had done through the night, and several times he halted and listened, casting watchful eyes this way and that. Sometimes he dismounted to examine hoof-marks on the soft ground. He was adept at reading signs that told him whether the horses that had passed recently were those of the troops, or farm animals. As far as possible he avoided meeting up with any other people, even if it was only with villagers. No one could really be trusted.

A couple of hours passed and Prudence began to feel hungry. They made good progress, and put several miles between them and the hut before Edward reined in beside a small rivulet where the horses could drink.

'We'll have some of that bread and cheese now,' he said.

She needed no second bidding to dismount, and quickly took out the food which she had wrapped in a clean linen cloth before she had left the hostelry. It was hardly a feast to relish, but it was wholesome, sustaining food and they both munched at it with the satisfaction of healthy appetites.

They spoke little, and soon they were riding on again. Darkness began softly to envelop the countryside, and still they rode on. The moon was high in the sky when they reached the coast. The track skirted mudflats, where sea-thrift and glass-wort grew, and the air was pungent with the salty smell of seaweeds.

Edward found a hostelry not far from the quay, where the horses could be watered, fed and stabled. Prudence booked a room for herself, and was glad to be able to attend to her personal toilet. Feeling much refreshed, she joined Edward in a private room where he had arranged for supper to be served for them both.

'I can hardly believe we're actually here, safe and sound,' she said.

A prayer of thanksgiving ran through her mind. That stage of the journey was over, and her thoughts turned to Nat and the wagon. She had been too preoccupied to spare much thought for him, or for her few goods, precious though they were. Now she began to worry as to whether Edward had been correct in his assessment of Nat's character. Would she ever see either of them again? If he stole everything where could she obtain replacements for all the goods that were packed in the wagon?

The voyage could take forty or fifty days, or even more if the ship met with misfortune. Each passenger had to take enough food to last for that period. It was always an important part of every housekeeper's work to ensure that her larder was well stocked before each winter. Prudence liked to do a good deal of the work herself, and was meticulous in overseeing that standards were kept by the maids who worked with her. Fortunately some of those goods had been stored in an outhouse which had escaped the fire that had destroyed their house. A friend of the family had kindly allowed Prudence the use of her kitchen so she could finish the salting, drying and smoking of a variety of foodstuffs. She also made potted meats, flavoured with herbs and carefully sealed with a thick layer of suet to keep the jars airtight. She had preferred to do as much as possible herself, not always trusting the care and cleanliness which others might use. In small barrels, boxes and clean linen wrapping, all these items had been neatly packed in the wagon. It would be a temptation for any poor man to take them—she could only hope that Nat was honest.

Her thoughts were diverted when the landlord himself carried in the meal—what was it about Edward that made people happy to serve him well? Was it simply because he expected good service that it was so readily and willingly given? She was too hungry to ponder the point. It was several hours since they had consumed the stale bread and cheese. Perhaps that was what made the fresh meat and vegetables in the dishes before them taste particularly delicious. With hearty appetites they both cleared the plates quickly, and drank the accompanying tankards of ale.

Biting into a juicy russet apple to finish his meal, Edward leaned back in his chair. 'What's the name of your ship?' he asked.

'The *Angelica*.'

She noticed how tired he looked, scarcely able to keep his eyes open, and remembered with gratitude how on the previous night he had kept watch so that she could sleep.

'We'll look for it first thing in the morning,' he promised her.

'Yes,' she agreed. 'It's far too late now to start a search.'

He finished the apple, yawned and stood up. 'I shall not impose my company upon you tonight. I shall find a corner of the snug in which to sleep.'

Was that because he was so tired, she wondered—or had her message of rejection reached him at last? She was furious with herself when she realised that she missed his company in the bedroom. She thumped the pillows hard and made a determined effort to get to sleep.

Side by side, they walked down the cobbled street and, only a short distance along it, came to the quayside. It was not yet breakfast-time at the inn, but Prudence had been too impatient to wait, and Edward agreed that they could return to the inn to eat later on. He was looking well refreshed and very alert, and was gazing about with intense interest. Early though it was, the town was thronging with people, the street and the quayside hustling and bustling with activity. There were several groups which looked as if they might be emigrants—two or three families together, some of which had servants with them. Many had obviously slept out, in or beneath their wagons; others must have simply lain on the hard ground. Women were handing out chunks of bread to their families, pouring out cups of small ale or milk, newly delivered by a vendor with churns strapped to a pack donkey.

'I see no sign of Nat—nor of your wagon,' Edward remarked after they had walked almost to the end of the quay.

Prudence bit her lip. She was anxious about that. Even if Nat was honest, he might have fallen foul of robbers.

'He would not risk travelling after dark,' she said, trying to convince herself. 'And it would take him longer with the wagon than it did for us to ride. I think he should get here later this morning.'

'Let us hope so!'

Thankfully just at that moment she noticed one vessel which was slightly larger than the others—a tall-masted ship, stoutly built of thick oak planks. Prudence hurried towards it until she could read the name—*Angelica*.

Edward followed her. 'She looks to be a tidy, seaworthy vessel,' he remarked.

She had no means of judging that. She was thinking that, although the ship was large compared to the rest of the fleet in dock, it seemed frail compared to the mightiness of the ocean. The gangplank was already in place, and men were carrying goods up on to the ship.

'They must be sailing soon—they've started loading,' Edward pointed out. 'And probably those are some of the people you've been trying to catch up with.'

She glanced around at the faces of those who were standing near by. One in particular seemed to be supervising the loading, and was obviously the leader of the expedition. He was clever-looking and sharp-featured, a man of average height, dressed entirely in black from his high-crowned hat to his wide breeches, woollen stockings and sturdy shoes. When he rapped out an order it was instantly obeyed. The other men and women stood patiently beside their bales and bundles, pieces of furniture, boxes and barrels, looking a little lost and hapless. Only the children seemed animated, playing some chasing and catching game that occasionally earned a clip on the ear from an irritated adult when it became too boisterous.

'That's Elias Smith,' she pointed the man in black out to Edward. 'He and his wife visited us a year ago when they first decided to charter a ship, and were beginning to make up a party to emigrate to New England. They wanted my father to say we would definitely go with them, but at that time he had not quite made up his mind.'

'Doubtless Master Smith will be pleased to know that you have arrived,' Edward remarked.

'I'll go and let him know——' She would have rushed straight across to Elias Smith, but Edward caught hold of her arm, swinging her round to face him.

'Make no mention of my presence here,' he instructed.

'But will you not come with me to meet him?'

'Have you forgotten I am a wanted man?' he said bitterly.

'Surely you are safe here?' Then impulsively she exclaimed, 'Why don't you sail with us, Edward?'

A smile flickered over his handsome face. 'An invitation? Have you come to like my company, Prudence?'

She tossed her head, refusing to admit it. 'It's not that. I was thinking of your safety.'

'My safety will best be ensured if my presence here is not known. I shall return to the inn. By the way, what do you propose to do about the horses, Prudence?'

'Whatever you wish.' She had no further need of them. 'They are yours now.'

'You paid for them——'

''Tis no matter.' They had indeed cost her quite a lot of money, but that was meaningless. Edward was not yet clear of pursuit—she was terrified that even yet something terrible might happen to him.

'I'll see to them,' he said. He walked briskly away. She watched him until he was lost to view among the throng on the quayside. There was a sadness deep inside her as she realised that soon she would be leaving so much that she loved. She took herself severely in hand as she also realised she was still thinking of him. She was acting like a fool. Edward had no such thoughts about being parted from her—that was quite clear. He had walked away with a positively jaunty step.

She had to look after herself and her own interests. She must make herself known to these strangers she was about to join, and sought to recognise the face of Mistress Smith among the women. She could not see that good lady, however, and there was no one else she knew. Elias Smith looked so very busy and had such a domineering manner that she hesitated. But that was only momentarily, then characteristically she squared her shoulders and approached him boldly.

'Master Smith—I'm Prudence Collins.' He waved past a man whose back was bent beneath the weight of a comb-sack of wheat, then turned and stared searchingly at her with cold grey eyes. She explained further, 'You visited my father, Jacob Collins, in Norwich some time ago. Recently our house was burned down and because of that we set off to join your convoy.'

'Mistress Collins. I do remember, indeed. I received your father's message. We've been looking out for you.' He took her hand in a firm grip. 'And where is your father?'

'I'm afraid—he—he's dead. We were attacked by robbers——'

'My poor young lady. How dreadful—dreadful.' He looked genuinely sympathetic. 'God rest his soul.'

'Amen to that. It was indeed horrifying, but I can't tell you about it now. I'm so glad I've found you before you sail.'

'You're just in time. We depart tomorrow on the early-morning tide. But surely you have not travelled here alone?'

'I have had help, but my friend—friends have had to continue their journey.'

'Could they not wait to see you off?' She shook her head. Elias broke off momentarily to give instructions, then turned to face her again. 'All luggage has to be taken on board today. You must bring your provisions here at once.'

'My wagon has not yet arrived,' she told him anxiously.

'We shall sleep on the ship tonight, ready to sail at dawn.' He stared down at her and his face was set in harsh lines. She thought he might refuse to take her unless she had adequate means to feed herself, and she was quite taken by surprise when he added, 'We have enough to feed one extra. You can accompany my family.'

'I would not wish to cause you to be short——' she objected.

'I have enough. I, too, have suffered a bereavement. My wife died a few days after we left home. You may eat her share.'

Prudence was shocked and saddened, not only by the news itself but by the matter-of-fact way in which he made the announcement. There was no flicker of emotion on his sharp face. 'I—I'm so sorry——' she stammered.

'It was God's will,' he said piously. 'You can earn your keep by looking after the children,' he added.

'I will be glad to do that,' Prudence said. A couple of men carrying a heavy chest between them asked for instructions. Perhaps Elias was deliberately keeping busy to cover the grief she was sure he must be feeling. Of course, she would be willing to help to look after his children, but she was not sure she wanted to spend too much time in the company of their father. She turned away, thinking that she would much prefer to travel independently, and with an element of desperation resumed her search along the quayside, trying to find Nat.

Then she saw him. He was running towards her. 'Mistress Collins,' he panted, 'I've just got here——'

'Nat. I'm so pleased to see you! Where's my wagon?' she asked.

'Back there. It's all safe and sound. 'But I've got bad news——'

'What . . .?' Her voice trailed away.

'The soldiers—they rode into town only a few minutes after I got here.'

Fear caught her in an iron grip. 'Were they from Tillington?'

'I believe so, Mistress.' He kept glancing anxiously over his shoulder. 'They mustn't find me here.'

'No, of course not. Bring the wagon here; I'll get help to unload it. Then you can leave at once.'

An expression of gratitude flashed over his face. He sped away and was back at once, whipping the horse along in a manner that would have distressed Prudence if she had not been so aware of the danger Nat had put himself in. How could she ever had doubted him?

Several men helped to unload the wagon, and immediately Nat turned the horse and trundled away—not back into the town, but taking a track that led away into the country. Prudence said a silent prayer that he would reach his home and his family safely.

Leaving Elias to see to the loading of her provisions, she lifted her skirts and ran along the quay in a manner that was exceedingly improper for any young lady, let alone one in Puritan garb. Did Edward know that the Roundheads had arrived and were searching for him?

She must warn him. She turned into the street, then realised that such haste was attracting unwelcome attention and forced herself to slow her steps to a quick walk. The Roundheads would undoubtedly be on the look-out for her, and have instructions to arrest her as well as Edward, though undoubtedly his capture would be their prime objective. She must hurry. He must leave Harwich with all possible speed.

She was too late. She checked her step as she saw Roundhead soldiers lounging around the doorway of the inn. She looked at all the faces: there was none she recognised, and that gave her a small measure of relief. Probably those who had allowed the prisoner to escape were now in gaol themselves. She had no sympathy for them—but would any of these men recognise her?

Her heart contracted with fear. Where was Edward? With eyes demurely downcast and her heart beating fast, she passed by the men and through the door. There were more soldiers inside— they had obviously descended on the town in considerable force. Undoubtedly Edward was a prize prisoner. She dared not look into any of the rooms, though she longed to know whether he might be there. She moved on up the stairs and into her bedroom. Her things were there in the saddlebags—the horse-pistol had gone. That fact told her nothing.

From her window she could see down into the stable-yard at the back. About twenty of the troopers' horses were tied up. It would be dangerous for her to go down and look into the stables. Any false movement might attract the soldiers' attention to her. She could not think what to do.

A knock on the door startled her. Cautiously she opened it. The landlord stood on the threshold and behind him was one of the Parliamentarian officers, his buff-coat crossed by the distinctive tawny orange sash. Three troopers accompanied him, their eyes as steely as their lobster-pot helmets, face-guards making their unfriendly faces more threatening.

'These gentlemen are searching every room, mistress.'

Prudence stepped aside. 'There is no one here except me,' she said. 'And I am due to leave immediately.'

'Where are you going, mistress?' asked the officer.

'To America,' she said, keeping her answer as brief as possible.

'What is your name?'

Were they looking for her or only for Edward. Should she use his name or her own? She had to make a quick decision. 'I am Mistress Collins,' she told him boldly.

She was relieved to see that that information did not cause a flicker on his expression.

The soldiers made a quick sweep of the room, peered beneath the bed and into a cupboard. There

was nowhere anyone could hide, but the captain
still regarded her suspiciously.

'It was said that the prisoner who escaped was
aided by a young woman,' he said. 'Have you any
proof that you are expected on this ship?'

'I have papers.'

'Papers mean nothing. Is there anyone from the
ship who will vouch for you?'

'The leader of the expedition is Elias Smith. He
knows me. I am to help in the care of his children,'
she said.

'Fetch this man,' ordered the captain. 'And bring
this woman down to my office.'

It seemed an age before Elias Smith appeared.
When he arrived at last he had obviously been
brought forcibly, reluctant to leave his task of
supervising the loading of the ship.

'Do you know this woman?' asked the captain.

'She is to travel with my expedition. I have already taken all her provisions on board.'

He was interrupted by a commotion outside the
door. It was flung open and a second officer strode
into the room, looking both important and triumphant. He saluted smartly, with an air of scarcely
suppressed excitement.

'Sir, we've recaptured the escaped prisoner. My
men are bringing him in to town. I rode ahead personally to let you know.'

Prudence felt her head swim; mist floated over
her eyes, consciousness began to slip away. Her
knees buckled beneath her. Vaguely she was aware

of Elias Smith's grasping her and swinging her over his shoulder as if she were nothing more than a sack of grain.

CHAPTER NINE

'PRUDENCE.'

The voice came to her as a sibilant whisper—was it a trick of the wind? She must be hallucinating—because she had thought so much about Edward she was now imagining she could hear his voice.

They had been at sea for five days, the *Angelica* had worked its way from Harwich, through the Channel, and its bow was headed westwards, beginning to breast the rolling waves of the Atlantic. Ahead of them lay a journey of three thousand miles, and the passengers were doing their best to settle down and adapt to the discomfort of cramped living-conditions. Prudence had been allocated a small corner below decks, beneath some sort of overhanging wooden structure—she had not yet discovered what it was. She had been dumped there unceremoniously by Elias Smith when he had carried her straight from the inn and on to the ship. He had settled her there among her own belongings, and given strict instructions that she was not to be allowed to leave.

There was no chance of disobeying. When she tried to go ashore, desperate to discover more information, she came up against a wall of opposition from the others in the group. They barred her way and made sure that their leader's orders were obeyed. On the morning tide the ship sailed, and she felt utterly defeated. Edward was again in the hands of the Roundheads, and they would make sure he did not get away a second time. They would hold a charade of a trial and he would be hanged. She could not bear to think of it; she screwed her eyes so tight closed that they hurt, trying to shut out that appalling vision, but it was imprinted on her mind. She thought of flinging herself overboard, but what would have been the use of that? In any event, for those first days she was so carefully watched that she doubted if she would have been able to do it anyway. Somehow she had to make herself accept that there was nothing she could do—and that she would never see him again in this world. Her agony was so intense that she could not cry, though tears would have been a relief.

Many of her fellow travellers wept unashamedly as the ship left port, shedding tears for the relatives and friends they were leaving behind, and for the old country in which they had been born, even though they had suffered persecution there. Perhaps, thought Prudence, if she had been leaving Edward behind, a free man, she would have been able to cry and come to terms with her future. It was the terrible knowledge that he had been recaptured that made her so distraught.

The Smith children had been her salvation, poor motherless little souls. She felt dreadfully sorry for them, remembering how desolate she had felt when her own mother had died. She had then been older than these little mites and, she thought grimly, she had had a more caring father too. There were four of them, three boys and one girl, whose ages ranged from ten down to two. The two older boys were well grown, and had been severely disciplined by their father. When he was not around they could burst out with just as much boisterous energy as the rest of the children on board. Prudence had organised the other parents to designate a space for the children's recreation area, where they could play simple games. She also undertook to give basic lessons in arithmetic, reading and writing, though the movement of the ship made that rather difficult. Everyone took turns to watch the children when they were on deck, being constantly in fear of their falling overboard.

Of the Smith family the youngest, five-year-old Susannah and little Peregrine, who was only two, were the ones who called for the most attention. Their needs ensured that they quickly made a place for themselves in Prudence's warm heart. Those two little ones turned to her as a mother-substitute almost immediately. Before long they were flinging themselves into her arms, rather than those of their father, when they suffered any accidental knocks and bruises.

'You are a great comfort and help to us all, Prudence,' Elias said to her on the fifth evening after they left Harwich.

'I am happy to be of some use,' she replied, 'for I have little to do during the voyage.'

'The children have grown fond of you already.'

'I'm glad of that.'

He was silent for a moment, then asked, 'What do you propose to do when we arrive in New England?'

She was surprised by his question. 'Why, then I shall hope to make myself useful to my uncle and his family.'

'I cannot help observing that my children are already beginning to look upon you as a mother,' he said.

She drew a little away from him, and made a guarded reply. 'How sad it must be for you, too, that you have lost your dear wife.'

He nodded, and she was conscious that he was watching her closely. His expression reminded her of that she had seen on one or two of the elders before. She wanted no involvement with Elias—to care for and even to love his children was one thing; for him, personally, she had absolutely no feeling. She certainly did not want to encourage any thought he might have that it could ever be otherwise. She stood up abruptly.

'I need some fresh air, Master Smith. The children will benefit from having your company to themselves for a time, while I take a turn around the deck.'

Stepping over and round the other passengers, some of whom had already laid out their bedding for the night, she made her way to the companion-ladder that led to the deck. The wooden ship creaked, its bow nosed into the Atlantic swell, and with a stiff breeze they were making good speed. One of the officers shouted an order, and Prudence had to stand well back as some of the men who were helping the sailors to manage the boat ran across the deck to work the sails. The great sheets of canvas made a loud flapping noise as they were hauled in a little. There was always noise on board, even at night, when most of the passengers were sleeping, as the work of sailing the ship continued.

'Prudence.'

There it was again—Edward's voice—but it couldn't be! Was it a ghost? She spun round . . . peered into the darkness . . . ran a step in the direction from which the sound had come—then stopped, choked with fear of the unseen. She turned back—and encountered a solid body, and there was absolutely nothing ghostly about the pair of strong arms that closed so tightly around her that she gasped.

'Shush!' he whispered, soothing and warning at the same time.

His breath swept her cheek. There was nothing ethereal in the feel, the warmth, the sweet musky smell of the man who held her. All those flooding sensations answered a deep longing in her—and yet she could not fully believe it.

'Edward?' she queried tentatively.

'Of course.' The voice still held the tinge of sardonic amusement.

'But . . . you were captured—weren't you?'

'I heard that rumour too. They'd got their hands on some poor wretch, but most definitely it was not me.'

'The officer said——' She paused, trying to remember just what he had said. Something so terrible that she had fainted—she knew that.

'Never mind what the officer said. I was already on board this vessel when that happened. I only hope they will have discovered their error by now and let the other fellow go.'

She drew back her head and stared up into his face, half hidden by shadow, trying to make out those features that had become so familiar to her over the days they had travelled together. In her estimation no one could possibly mistake Edward for any other.

'How did you get on board?' she asked, but she did not really care. He was here—that was the important thing; he was safe, not dangling at the end of a rope as she had supposed.

'I've some experience at sailing,' he replied laconically. 'The captain was in need of a mate, especially someone who can chart the ship's course by the stars.'

'Can you do that?'

He laughed at her incredulity. 'Of course. That would not be something I would lie about. To get it wrong could put the whole ship in jeopardy, myself included.'

Of course, she should have known. He was always so competent, and she had total faith in his ability. Whatever he undertook he did thoroughly and well. If any man could get them safely to America it would be Edward. That thought brought Prudence fully to her senses so that she remembered where they were and that, although they were in a shadowy corner, the ship was crowded. While she had absorbed the wonderful knowledge that he was alive and well, she had remained standing locked in his arms, and had been delighted to be held there so firmly. She really ought to pull herself out of his embrace. She moved back slightly, unwillingly, motivated only by her rigid moral principles. He loosened his hold, but did not entirely release her.

'You could have let me know earlier that you were safe,' she objected. 'Did you not know how concerned I was?'

'Were you? You did not show it.'

'What would have been the point? I thought you were dead.' Then, realising what he had said, she stepped back, and his arms fell to his sides. 'You mean you have been observing me, in secret? Without catching my attention?'

'A delightful picture you presented, playing with your adopted family.' He paused, then, with a harsher note in his voice, continued, 'I've watched you talking with their father—a widower, I understand.'

'He is,' she replied crisply. 'I have undertaken to care for his young family during the voyage.'

'He is obviously a man of substance.'

'I believe so,' she shrugged.

'And one of your own kind.'

'We are both Puritans,' she agreed.

'That is most evident.' The mockery was back in his voice.

'Everyone knows that most of the settlers in America are of the same persuasion.'

'Exactly,' he sighed. 'There are times when I wonder just what I am letting myself in for over there.'

He would never have left England, never have boarded the *Angelica* if he had not been a wanted man. He had joined them to save his life, she knew that. They all had their various reasons for being there, tossed about on the high seas. 'The future is veiled for all of us,' she said.

'But you know precisely what your life will be.' There was a bitter note in his voice. 'You will be taken into your uncle's household and soon you will be married. Did you not tell me so?'

'It is quite probable,' she replied. She kept her voice cool and level, though the thought of marriage to a stranger was not one she now welcomed.

'You will make a lovely young wife—and mother,' he said.

Obviously he was teasing her again—laughing at her. When he did that her pleasure at being with him was clouded. It had been an infinity of joy to know that he was here and safe. Wonderful, too, to be held for those brief moments in his arms, to feel the throb of his heart against her breast. That was entirely physical—but oh, how powerful it had been! Her awareness of him had been so intense that she had felt as if her whole being, body and soul, had been absorbed into his.

Momentarily she had deluded herself into believing that he felt the same way, that he cherished her as she did him. Now she had to admit that there was no real accord between them, no communion of spirit. The gulf that had yawned between them, separating their lives from their very first encounter, was just as wide as—perhaps even wider than—before. He was a Cavalier, a King's man, with all that implied of arrogance, inherited wealth and lordly disdain. She had to remain a Puritan—

she had been born and brought up among those good people. She must not weaken—must not change. She would not—unless he called her. If only he wanted her as a wife—and mother...

She shook that impossibly wicked thought away. She might as well cry for the moon. She had to say something rational, and was glad that her voice came from her dry mouth steadily. 'I understand the settlement has grown considerably since the first pilgrims arrived there. I am sure you will find others who are of your way of thinking.'

'I do not propose to advertise my "way of thinking", as you call it,' he told her. 'I am Edward Hayward now, as plain a man as ever you are likely to come across.'

What foolish talk was that? Did he not realise that nothing about him was plain? His aristocratic upbringing was there in every inch of him, in the proud way he held his head, the uncompromisingly straight line of his nose, and the firm determination of his chin. To her there would never be any man who could match him in looks—though temperamentally he was one of the most difficult she had ever come across.

'Prudence,' he appealed to her seriously, 'I trust that you will forget anything you may have heard regarding titles and land as readily as you forgot my clothing when we first met. I want no complications when we arrive in America.'

'You had my promise before. I give it again willingly now,' she said.

'Thank you.' He picked up her hand and gave it a friendly squeeze.

'Shall we speak together again?' she asked.

'It will be difficult to avoid it, since it is such a small ship.'

'That is true.' They were being agonisingly polite now. She would have liked an assignation, but he offered nothing.

'Now I must go and mark the position of the stars on the charts,' he said. 'I shall see that you get to America safely. Goodnight, Prudence.'

He left as suddenly and unexpectedly as he had arrived. She shivered as if the night air had turned colder, and she felt somehow vulnerable. She turned and descended the ladder into the overcrowded, stuffy area twixt decks. The Smith children were all asleep. Elias appeared to be waiting for her return.

He stood up and whispered, 'I was growing anxious for you, Prudence. I was about to come in search of you.'

'There was no need for that.' She was angry that he should have thought it necessary.

He gave her a sharp glance. He was not accustomed to having his views questioned. 'In future I must ask you not to stay away from the children so long.'

'You were with them,' she observed, just managing to keep her temper.

'That is so—on this occasion.'

She brushed past him. She had no wish to enter into conversation with him, wanting only to be alone with her thoughts, to drop down and crawl into that corner that was her own private space.

Elias caught hold of her, slipped an arm around her waist and drew her towards him. 'I was worried—and lonely—without you,' he murmured.

'Master Smith—I beg you—let me go,' she hissed at him with a feeling of intense repugnance. She squirmed, trying to free herself without making an embarrassing commotion that would wake the whole ship.

'Lie down here—beside me,' he whispered insistently in her ear. Then to her horror he tried to knock her legs from beneath her so that he could drag her to the floor where his bed-roll was spread out.

Alarmed, she struck out at him and, caught off balance as the ship rolled, she staggered. She half fell over the sleeping form of Susannah and just managed to avoid landing on top of the child, but she could not help wakening her.

'Mamma—Mamma!' The little girl awoke, screaming.

'Hush, darling. I'm here. You're all right.' She cuddled the shaking child in her arms, and at the same time moved as far away from Elias as the overcrowded conditions would allow. He had the sense not to press himself on her further.

When Susannah was again asleep Prudence curled up in her corner. It was not the encounter with Elias that remained in her mind, but the relief of knowing that Edward was alive. That was so wonderful, and for the first time on the voyage so far she drifted off to sleep without anxiety.

*   *   *

When Edward left Prudence he made his way down to the captain's cabin, where the charts were spread out on the polished oak table. He had to make his regular check on the position of the *Angelica*. On the wide Atlantic, far from sight of land, there were only the stars to guide them. He had noted those that were visible, and from that observation would make an estimate of their course and confirm this at noon the following day, after marking the whereabouts of the sun. It was inexact at the best of times, but there was no other known method. That evening he was convinced that they were well on the way and heading in the right direction. Whether he would be as confident tomorrow, when the impending storm was raging, he was not so sure.

Should he have warned Prudence that they were running into rough weather? He had been about to, but he was not absolutely sure. It was just possible that he had misread the signs, and he had no wish to cause her to worry unnecessarily. He gave a wry smile at his own foolishness. He never seemed able to think straight when she was near.

He had broken the vow he had made when he'd come on board. He had determined then that he would remain remote from her—but at the first temptation he had weakened. He relived the moment when he'd seen her there, looking out at the rolling ocean, and standing so close to him that he could smell the sweet cleanliness of her. In that moment he had been unable to control himself. Every masculine instinct he possessed had urged him to reach out and clasp her tight to his chest, to feel the soft warmth of her shapely young body and press her hard against himself. So as not to frighten her unduly he had called her name softly, twice over. Her response to that, the way she had seemed to hold her breath while she had turned her head this way and that, listening and looking, had told him that she was eager to find him—the very thought of it made his pulses race and throb. What a fool he was!

She was a sweet kind-hearted maid. It pleased him to know how concerned she had been for his safety. He recalled thinking once how fascinating it would be to discover what emotions were hidden beneath her plain Puritanical dress. He knew rather more now—he had felt the loveliness of the body that was so straight and slender and delicately curving. It pleased him to allow his mind to dwell on that. He knew too that she thought him flippant, and so he was in his dealings with her. How else could he protect himself from the magic her presence could so easily spin around him? When he was with her he was like a spider caught in her web—and it was not a web that he liked.

She had not changed. She never would change. She was Puritanical in every aspect of her life. Granted that some of those virtues were generally considered to be highly commendable, they were damnably uncomfortable to his way of thinking, and not what he was used to. Such sentiment had little to do with the pleasures of life. Why the devil did he bother about her? He knew perfectly well that she would never be happy with a man such as he. If it had been only a bit of dalliance... What was he thinking of? He put an abrupt ban on that line of thought. He had never in his life before entered into any relationship with a woman that could not be shelved under the category of ephemeral. Why should he change his lifestyle now?

Again he chided himself for being a fool. He knew very well that Prudence belonged to those who had fashioned her in their mould. It would be a kindness to leave her there—and he owed her no less, for she had put herself in great danger when she had rescued him from gaol. Poor thanks it would be for him now to drag her off into the wilderness, to live the hard life of a planter. What did he know of husbandry in this strange land they were sailing to? In all probability he would starve to death in the first winter. He had nothing to offer a woman. He must stifle his longings.

The storm raged for days on end. The ship pitched and rolled in the mountainous seas, the wind shrieked like a horde of dervishes through the rigging, even though the sails were reefed down. It was impossible for any of the women or children to go on deck, as giant waves broke over the sides and covered the ship in a sheet of white foam. Every stitch of canvas had been taken in, and the ship drifted with as little control as if it were a piece of driftwood. It pitched down into the troughs of the waves so that many thought they were going to the bottom of the ocean, then it was lifted up on to their crests, with water streaming over the gunwales. The passengers were flung about like corn in a sieve. Prudence was too concerned with keeping the children safe from injury, and cleaning them up when they were sick, to have time left to worry much. Their safety was in the hands of the Lord, and she took comfort in the knowledge that Edward was there as one of the ship's officers to help Him. He had said that they would reach America safely, and her belief in his capability was such that she felt assured that, if it was humanly possible for the ship to come through these terrible seas without mishap, Edward would manage it.

For most of that time the fires in the galley were washed out and could not be relighted, so it was impossible to have hot meals. Prudence was glad of the potted meats she had prepared so carefully in her kitchen back in Norwich. She opened some jars of pressed ox-tongue and generously shared the meat around as far as it would go. Cooking was impossible for several days.

Then at last the storm abated a little, and the relief was immense. The galley stove was relit, fresh bread baked, and some cod, caught by the sailors, enabled them to have a meal that seemed as good as a feast. It had been impossible to wash and dry clothes too, and even the bedding was damp, and on the very first fine day so much laundry-work was carried out and there were so many shirts and shifts and boothose strung up across the deck that the ship looked as if it had been bedecked in bunting.

During the storm there had been no chance for Prudence to speak to Edward. Now that it was calmer she hoped there might be an opportunity to meet again, and cherished the thought that in the evening she would be able to go up on deck and wait at the same place as before. Somehow she was sure he would come to her there.

She did not have to wait as long as that before she saw him again. It was late morning, and she was hanging out the clothes she had just washed for herself and the children when she became aware of him. Joy rushed into her heart and she smiled in his direction. Edward was lounging idly against a barrel. In her opinion he certainly deserved some relaxation, for it must have been very hard work to have brought them all safely through the storm — then with something of a shock she realised he was not alone. He was engaged in conversation with a young woman, whose bright auburn hair escaped from beneath her white cap, which did not look anything like as demure as it should have done. In fact it was perched at an exceedingly provocative angle on the back of her head.

Prudence pursed her lips together to smother the gasp of displeasure that might have burst out audibly. She glanced away quickly, pretending she had not noticed, and entered into a positive fury of activity, wringing the last drops of water from one of the boy's shirts. She flapped it vigorously open and concentrated hard upon the task of fastening it securely to one of the ropes. As she'd been doing his children's washing Elias had handed her some shirts and his long linen night-shift, almost as if he were conferring an honour upon her. She had felt obliged to scrub them for him, though she had little keenness for the task, and had not been sorry when the strength of her rubbing had produced a rather large hole. Probably he would expect her to mend it as well, she thought grimly.

The night-shift now looked so ragged that she was ashamed of it, and tried to find somewhere inconspicuous to hang it. Just then the wind tugged at it with such force that it was flicked out of her hands and blown straight towards Edward. In a flash one of his hands shot out and he caught it.

'Oh, you caught that a treat, sir.'

The young woman clapped her hands enthusiastically. Prudence recognised her as Marjorie Sampson, the eldest daughter of one of the less devout families. Several of the women had remarked that the girl's mother really ought to make her a new dress, for she had a well-rounded figure, and the gown she wore every day except Sundays seemed to stretch so tightly that her bosom threatened to burst out of the narrow black bodice, pushed up by the constricting corset beneath. She appeared to be on very familiar terms with Edward.

Edward held up Elias's embarrassing garment, waved it in the direction of Prudence and, striding towards her, made a ceremonious bow.

'Yours, I believe,' he said.

The gesture was so openly friendly that Prudence chided herself for having that ridiculous pang of jealousy, and she smiled warmly in return. She was made even happier to find that he appeared to be in no hurry to leave her side. They conversed for a few minutes more, about the power and the drama of the storm and the relief of coming through it without serious damage or loss. Her heart was lightened as she returned below, for she had more domestic chores to attend to. Although he had not suggested an assignation, somehow she was convinced that this evening they would meet again, just as they had before the storm.

She hurried on with her work, and was pleased to be able to cook again, making a really appetising and sustaining meal for them all. Elias ate with especial satisfaction and thanked her very much for all her trouble. She had kept a cool attitude towards him, and, although she could tell he was still attracted to her, she was grateful that he made no more advances. There was no way she could avoid spending quite a lot of time with him because of her commitment to the children. They had grown more dear to her with every passing day, and it was now over six weeks since they had left England behind.

She was a little concerned that the younger two might be getting too dependent on her, but pushed that thought out of her head. Life on board ship was obviously very different from what it would be when they arrived in the new colony. She took care to let Elias know quite positively that when they arrived in New England she intended to move in with her uncle and aunt, who were elderly and would, she was sure, be glad of her assistance.

Elias had nodded his head with friendly understanding. 'None of us can know for certain what will confront us when we arrive,' he said. 'I set out with the intention that together my wife and I would help my brother, Philamon. He has never married, and now that he is getting on in years he will dearly love having me and my family around to look after him and to whom he can leave his possessions. He will be saddened and disappointed to learn that my wife is no longer with us.'

'It is good to know that we are both sailing towards a useful and satisfying life,' Prudence said. She tried very hard to make herself believe that she would want nothing better—only to find her best intentions challenged by the intrusion of a mental picture of Edward's face and mocking smile. She sighed. How much better it would be if she could share the future with him!

'I've been told we have only a few days' more sailing before we sight land, Prudence.' Elias broke into her daydream.

Her heart leapt. 'Why, Master Smith—that's wonderful news! Why haven't you said so before? Does everybody know?'

He put a finger to his lips. 'I shall announce it at prayers this evening, so that we may give special praise to the Lord.'

'Amen,' she responded, her eyes shining. 'It will be wonderful to feel the firm earth beneath my feet——'

He caught hold of her hand, interrupting her. 'Prudence, I must speak before we arrive, for we may then be parted for some time. You will be going to your uncle's home and I to my brother's. I do not know how far apart their holdings may be, but, however distant and difficult it is, I shall certainly visit you, and I want you to know that I intend to ask your uncle for your hand in marriage——'

'Master Smith—I beg you——'

'Say nothing more now, my dear girl. I was too precipitate before. It was quite right and proper for you to defend your virtue. I respect you for it, and it would not have been seemly to have made a match during the voyage, especially since we are both in mourning. But when we are again on God's good earth it will be a different matter. My brother assures me that he believes his holding to be the biggest in the settlement. I shall be able to assure your good relatives that I can provide for you——'

'Enough, Master Smith. Have done. I have no wish to wed——'

He gave her hand a conspiratorial squeeze. 'I understand, my dear. I shall not press you further until you are safe in the bosom of your family and in a position to receive a proper proposal.'

She withdrew her hand sharply. She was eager to go up on deck in the hope of meeting Edward. If she did not go up soon he might think she was not coming, especially as there had been no firm commitment. Rather than enter into a protracted and probably pointless argument with Elias she was content to leave the matter. She was sure that when she explained her feelings to her uncle and aunt they would convey them properly to Elias and she would be free of his attentions.

'I shall take a stroll on the deck, to breathe in the evening air,' she announced, wasting no more time.

'Do not be too long, Prudence,' he cautioned her.

She ignored that and hurried along the companion-ladder. She had to wait while a man descended, and chafed with impatience. Then swiftly, with the agility of youth and good health, she made her way up. It was only a few short steps to that place where she had stood on the evening before the storm. That hallowed place where she had discovered that Edward was very much alive and well, when he had clasped her in his arms. The sensation had been so delightful that the very memory of it made her heart start racing——

There was a movement in the shadows. She hesitated. Dared she speak his name? 'Edward?' She whispered it so softly that her voice was drowned in the noise as one of the sails flapped and some sailors rushed across the deck to deal with it.

The moon came out from behind a cloud and she saw that it was not Edward who stood there. It was Marjorie Sampson, and her red hair rippled seductively down her shoulders—obviously, she was expecting someone to join her. With an ache that was like a physical lump in the centre of her body, Prudence turned away.

CHAPTER TEN

'LAND ahoy!'

Prudence was on deck with the children when the cry came from the crow's nest.

'Land ahoy!' It was taken up by everyone who heard it, and the joyous shout echoed around the ship. Like a stone sending ripples over a pond, spreading in widening circles, it was repeated again and again.

'Where?'

'Let me see.'

Prudence lifted little Peregrine on to her hip, and, holding on tight to Susannah's hand, moved towards the bow, looking forward. She could hardly contain her excitement. What a relief it would be to stand on static solid ground again. Other passengers jostled around her, not unkindly but because they were so excited, so relieved. They could hardly believe it was true. They all wanted to see for themselves, to be among the first to sight this precious piece of earth and rock and fertility where they would be making their homes. With people crowding around her and the roll of the ship, Prudence almost lost her balance. She stumbled, and clutched the child in her arms to keep him safe, while the other was clinging to her hand.

'Steady. You'll get knocked over in the rush.'

Edward was immediately behind her, and his hands closed on her waist, holding her firmly. She could feel his breath on the nape of her neck.

She turned to face him, her eyes shining. 'Oh, Edward—is it really true? Are we there at last?'

'Almost. By my reckoning that should be Cape Cod lying just ahead of us.'

She craned her neck, staring forward, and was disappointed. 'I can't see anything.'

'Only the look-out can see land at the moment, but don't worry. It's there all right.' His hands were still holding her waist, and he leaned over her shoulder, pointing forward and a little to starboard. 'You'll see it first in that direction.'

He moved his head and his cheek brushed hers, the touch so gentle and intimate that she felt just as if she had been kissed. Her heart raced so fast that it frightened her. She froze warily. Did he think he could make advances both to her and to that Marjorie Sampson? Her head told her to take care, even though her heart was behaving so ridiculously. He was a typical Cavalier. She had known that when she had first met him, but recently her foolish emotions had almost deluded her into thinking he might be different. Now she reacted angrily and sharply, stepping aside and turning her head away.

As she did so she saw Elias making his way through the throng towards her. His face looked stormy, and she had no doubt he had noticed that Edward had his hands on her waist, and that he had almost kissed her. It was none of his business, but nevertheless she was deeply embarrassed—

shamed even. Elias pushed past her, making her move forward. Edward was compelled to remove his hands from her waist as Elias placed himself squarely in between them.

'Prudence—I do not think you should have brought the little ones up here. There are too many people about, and the children could be injured. Take them to the play-area below.'

'We were here when the cry went up,' she protested. 'I assure you the children are perfectly safe.' She paused, then added with cool disdain, 'if you think they should go below, by all means take them.' She held little Peregrine towards his father, and the child yelled in protest.

Elias glared at her and brushed the little boy aside. 'I cannot go below. I have to lead the assembly in prayers,' he snapped.

She was not surprised. Elias had given very little time to caring for his children and had been only too happy to leave their well-being entirely to her.

Stern-faced and angry, Elias turned to Edward. 'Master Hayward, can you confirm positively that we are within sight of the coast of New England?'

A slight smile played around the corners of Edward's mouth. He looked entirely at ease, untroubled by the barely suppressed fury that emanated from Elias. But somehow Prudence felt the enmity that had flared between the two men, almost as if it were a tangible barrier between them. And she knew that, quite unwittingly, she was at the centre of it.

'You may trust the word of the look-out,' Edward answered in his most haughty manner. 'He has most certainly sighted land.'

'America?' Elias demanded.

'I believe it to be Cape Cod.'

Other people around picked up this additional piece of information. It meant that they were well on course. Excitement increased as news of their location buzzed from one to another.

Elias drew himself up to bring their attention back to himself, as their leader. He raised his arms high and wide, as if reaching towards heaven. 'Good folk—let us kneel and offer up our thanks to God.'

Like corn falling before the reaper, the passengers dropped to their knees, many of them so overcome with emotion that tears rolled down their cheeks, and an audible wailing rose from more than one of them. Elias was delighted with their response. He remained standing, with his arms upraised, waiting for them all to settle and quieten.

Prudence began to move away, but now he stopped her. 'If you do not wish to go below, Prudence,' he said sharply, 'kneel here by my side, with my children.'

She was more than willing to kneel in thanksgiving, but disliked the proprietorial air which Elias assumed as an automatic right. She allowed her eyes to stray towards Edward. She had known he would be watching her, and felt a boiling sense of outrage. Neither of these men had any right to put pressure on, to try to influence her the way they were doing. The conflict between them threatened to engulf her.

It was not of her choosing, but somehow they were forcing her to make a decision.

Quickly but coolly she thought it over. When they arrived in New England she would have the protection of her uncle from the unwelcome advances of Elias, but only she could protect herself from the magic that Edward was capable of weaving around her. On no account must she allow him to sweep her off her feet. That could lead to nothing but misery—even though she seemed so inescapably drawn towards him. For her own peace of mind—and safety—she did what she had no wish to do. She knelt beside Elias, though she carefully placed both the small children between herself and him.

The harbour was sizeable, the mouth of a river that discharged into the sea, tucked back behind a long peninsula. It was deep enough to accommodate considerable ships, and several wharfs and a shipyard had been built. The wooden skeletons of boats in the process of construction stood on props. The settlement had already established a good fishery: three or four boats were tied up, and some of the women were busily salting their catch so that it would keep into the winter.

The news of the approach of the *Angelica* had reached the settlement two days earlier, at about the same time as the emigrants had sighted land. A flurry of excitement had brought women rushing from their houses, men from the fields, children from the schoolroom, timber-fellers in from the woods, and even the fishermen had turned back more quickly than usual. Not many new settlers had been able to leave England since the Civil War had begun, and almost certainly there would be no more boats from the old country until the early summer next year.

The people on shore waited with patience, aware of the time it needed for the approach to be made safely, but also with joy and expectation. Some, like Benjamin and Sarah Collins, were awaiting relatives; others simply hoped for news from family and friends at home. There would be letters on board, and useful goods. They were almost self-sufficient, but there were some things they had not yet been able to make or find substitutes for. Most of all, it was the contact with the old country that they longed for.

From the time the ship was first sighted there was always a knot of people gathered by the quayside. When it drew nearer the numbers increased so that everyone was there to witness its arrival, except for one woman who was in childbirth, and attended by another acting as midwife. Even one old man with a broken leg was carried out to the porch of his house so that he could see.

Edward was engaged with the captain in bringing the ship in safely. Prudence found her gaze travelling towards him more often than she would have liked ... Would their lives be totally severed after today? That thought clouded her pleasure in arriving at last in the New World. She had little time to think about it, however, for Elias had as usual left his children entirely to her charge. The boys were being difficult to control—the older two found

it impossible to stand still and leapt about like
crickets, off one foot and on to the other, despite
her admonitions to stand still. The younger children
were upset by the change in routine, by the nervous
buzz of excitement among the other passengers, and
they clung closely to her for reassurance. She felt
some anxiety for them—they had become so attached to her and they might not easily turn once
again to strangers. Elias was more in his element
as the leader of the party than he was as a father.

When at last they dropped anchor in the harbour
they lay so close that she could see the settlement
clearly. It consisted of a row of wooden houses,
some quite large, others simple cabins, but together they made a sort of street. Fields and
meadows stretched around them, and beyond were
junipers and pines and great oak trees, whose leaves
were sporting autumn hues of yellow and brown.
The day was fine, but there was a definite chill in
the air.

It seemed a welcoming sort of place. Most of the
people were waving and shouting; those on the ship
who recognised friends or relatives yelled out
greetings long before there was any chance of being
heard. Even before the ship's boat could be
lowered, several rowing boats came out to greet
them and everyone worked together in the slow
process of disembarking the passengers and their
luggage. The first of the emigrants to set foot on
the soil of New England were eagerly clasped in the
arms of loved ones. Prudence stood back, with
Peregrine in her arms and Susannah twisting at her
skirt. She was thankful that they had all arrived

safely, but felt no urgency to leave the ship, although there was no way she could stop the older boys from rushing on to one of the little boats at the very first opportunity. She was content to wait until Elias was ready to leave, and he was busy organising the departure of the rest of the company.

She saw the Sampsons disembark, an untidy family group, and as they reassembled on the quayside Marjorie turned and waved to someone on the ship. Prudence had no doubt she was waving to Edward, though she refused to look round to check on it, telling herself it was no concern of hers. It irked her and made her admit that subconsciously she had been hanging back in the hope of speaking to Edward once more before they parted. What a fool she was! Better to go ashore at once, she decided with a feeling of pique, and, taking the children, began to move towards the side of the ship ready to disembark.

'Allow me to take the little girl.' Edward was suddenly beside her, and scooping up a happily chuckling Susannah, he lowered her into the waiting arms of one of the seamen below. Prudence had to be grateful for his help with the children and in descending the ladder herself.

'Thank you,' she said, a trifle stiffly, as she settled in the boat with the children on either side of her. Then she added apologetically, 'I'm afraid Elias is busy.'

Edward had taken his seat opposite her. His lip curled. 'Seeing to everyone except his own family, I notice. These children would have had an awful time on the journey but for you, Prudence.'

She had no wish to enter into a discussion on the failings of Elias as a parent, though they were obvious enough. She simply shrugged dismissively. 'I was happy to look after them.'

'Yes, I believe you were,' he replied thoughtfully. 'Motherhood becomes you, Prudence.'

The intimate note in his voice was disturbing. She had noticed before that he always seemed to mean more than he actually said. She pretended she had not heard, and, remembering the cheeky wave Marjorie had just exchanged with him, she turned her face away. Susannah was staring ahead, asking questions, and Prudence was glad to busy herself with the little girl—and suddenly quite eager to take her first steps on American soil. It was a strange sensation not to feel the rolling of the ship beneath her feet.

'Oh, how good it is to be on dry land at last!' she exclaimed.

'It takes a bit of getting used to,' Edward agreed. He looked around with interest, standing firmly, with his long strong legs placed slightly apart. 'Have you seen your uncle and aunt yet, Prudence?'

'I've no way of recognising them,' she said.

'And they certainly won't be expecting you to be surrounded by a young family,' he remarked. 'I'll ask for you. Come with me, Susannah.'

He swung a very willing little girl high, and settled her comfortably on his broad shoulders. She sat there, blissfully sucking her thumb, as he strode over to greet a group of older people among whom were two men and a woman, all in their late fifties or early sixties.

He held a brief conversation with them, and immediately they all turned their heads to look in her direction. A few more words and they began to move forward, maintaining their solemn, steady dignity as respectable elders. One of the men was of about the same height as her father had been, dressed in Puritan fashion, with a grey goatee beard. The woman was tall and thin; she held herself proudly upright, and her face was narrow and deeply lined. There was no smile on her thin lips or in her cold hazel eyes. The trio came to a halt, facing Prudence.

'This is sad news you bring, Prudence,' said the woman. She did not introduce herself, but it was evident that she was Aunt Sarah. 'We had been so much looking forward to seeing your father again.'

'Very, very sad,' Prudence acknowledged with heartfelt simplicity. She dropped a little curtsy in deference to each of her relatives in turn. She could not help wishing there had been more warmth in the greeting, but, of course, they had been shocked by the news.

'Master and Mistress Collins were so astonished to see you alone, as well as surrounded by children, that I thought it wise to break the news to them,' Edward said by way of explanation. 'This gentlemen is Master Philamon Smith, the brother of Elias.'

'Good day to you, Master Smith,' Prudence greeted him also. She felt more welcomed by him than she had by her own relatives.

Elias had left the ship at last and, calling the two older boys to fall into step behind him, he walked smartly across. Unsmilingly the two men embraced each other. Prudence stood little Peregrine down, and gently but firmly Edward placed Susannah beside him, close to their older brothers.

'I'm so sorry to hear your tragic news, Elias,' said Philamon Smith.

'It was God's will,' Elias said devoutly. Then he turned to his children, lined them up and called out the names of each, starting with the eldest, and instructed them to bow or curtsy to their uncle.

Prudence noticed that Edward moved back a few steps, allowing the families to meet each other. No doubt he thought he had done his final duty by her and handed her over to her relatives. She waited patiently while their formal greetings were attended to. It had been a long and hazardous journey to make for such a cold reception at the end. Her uncle and aunt were both strangers to her, and she could not help reflecting on how different it would have been if her father had been here with her.

Uncle Benjamin entered into a conversation with Philamon Smith, speaking to him with deference on some matter of business. She very soon learned that their two holdings lay side by side and that the one owned by Philamon was indeed the largest in the settlement. The two men were elders of the Church, Philamon was also the leader of the community, and respect was shown to both by the other townspeople. Servants hovered in the background, awaiting orders, and a few minutes later were instructed to start carrying up the luggage to the respective houses.

Edward moved forward to rejoin the group. 'May I ask if there is an inn or hostelry in the township?' he asked.

'Not as there would be in England,' said Benjamin. 'But any of the folk here will put up a stranger.'

'Perhaps Master Hayward could stay with you, Uncle, until he is able to make his own arrangements?' Prudence was emboldened to ask. 'I owe him a debt of gratitude, for he defended me when my father was killed by the outlaws. Without his assistance I would never have got here.'

Her aunt's cold eyes swept over Prudence then flashed sharply back to Edward. 'Do you intend to settle here in the township?' she asked him.

'Only temporarily,' Edward replied. 'I've been told that a new settlement is being opened up not far from here. I believe that must be where my future lies and I should like to join those people and clear land for myself.'

Philamon Smith put a friendly hand on Edward's shoulder. 'I'm glad to hear you say that. You're just the sort of strong young man we're seeking to help open up the wilderness,' he said. 'A group of planters have already made a small start at clearing the forest further inland, but there is space for many, many more. I shall call a meeting in a couple of weeks' time. Then you can make up your mind. Meanwhile I suggest you accept Mistress Collins's kind invitation and stay with her.'

Aunt Sarah, who had never actually issued any invitation, looked stony-faced, but Philamon Smith was obviously too important a man to be argued with. 'I suppose you are in need of food?' she asked.

'We shall be glad of a meal, when it is convenient.' Prudence would have liked to refuse, but honesty and a rumbling stomach made that impossible. 'Our stocks were getting very low, and as we've been much engaged in preparing to leave the ship there has been no opportunity to light the fires for cooking these past two days.'

'Then let us make our way up to the house,' said Aunt Sarah. 'I'll give the servants instructions to prepare a simple repast.'

Prudence handed the children over to Elias, kissing each of the little ones as she did so.

'It's not a real parting,' Elias objected. 'If your uncle and aunt can spare you I shall be grateful for you to spend as much time as possible with the children.'

'I'll certainly visit them—but I think it would be better if you made other arrangements for their care as soon as you can.'

'Mistress Collins——' it was her aunt that he was appealing to '—I'm sure you can see how difficult it will be for me to manage without Prudence's help. I shall be everlasting grateful if you will allow her to spend some time with my family. They have become utterly devoted to her while we have been on board.'

'But of course, Master Smith.' Aunt Sarah was almost gushing. 'Prudence will have no special duties as far as I am concerned, and if it will be service to you and Philamon it will be a pleasure for me to be able to help.' Her gaze rested sternly on Prudence. 'I am sure you will be only too willing to continue to assist.'

Prudence could only bow her head with resignation. Was there no way she could escape from the unwelcome advances of Elias Smith?

Sarah Collins was delighted with the arrangement, obviously feeling that the presence of Prudence in the Smith household gave her added status. There was no way out of it, and the very next morning she was escorted personally by her Aunt Sarah to Philamon Smith's house. The two homesteads lay about half a mile apart, linked by a well-worn path. Aunt Sarah was a brisk walker, but Prudence had no difficulty in keeping up with her, though she would have liked to linger a little to take in the prettiness of the countryside around them. The open fields and the woods beyond called out to be explored, and about halfway along there was a small stream. It was crossed by a wooden footbridge, and was of great importance, being the fresh-water supply for the settlement, while further downstream the women used it for washing.

As they neared the house a door opened and the children—all four of them—came bursting out. 'Prudence—Prudence!' cried Susannah. 'I didn't think you'd ever come.'

She leapt up and Prudence swung her high in the air. Their joy and relief at seeing her was quite touching. How could she have thought of leaving them?

A motherly-looking middle-aged woman followed the children out of the kitchen. 'They've been so upset at being parted from you, Mistress Collins,' she said. 'Poor motherless little mites, transported all this way and then sent away with strangers.' She shook her head ruefully. 'I've done my best, but they've been longing to see you.'

'But their father was with them——' Prudence began.

Aunt Sarah interrupted her, appearing to disapprove of this chatter with servants. 'Where is Master Smith?' she demanded. 'I should just like to let him know you are here, then I must get back and be about my own business.'

'Master Philamon and Master Elias are both in the parlour,' said the woman, whose name turned out to be Martha Spinks, though Aunt Sarah did not introduce Prudence. In a low voice, for Prudence's ear only, she added disparagingly, 'Their father knows no more about children than the back end of a cow.'

'Come with me, Prudence,' instructed Aunt Sarah.

She marched into the house, and Prudence stood Susannah down and ruffled an affectionate hand through Peregrine's hair. 'I'm just going to see your uncle and your father. Then I'm going to spend all the rest of the day with you. Be good, now.'

'Don't be long, Prudence,' wailed Susannah.

'I'll be back in two shakes of a lamb's tail,' she promised.

She followed Aunt Sarah through the kitchen, which was well stocked with gleaming pots and pans that must have been brought out from England. A passageway led to a large room at the front of the house; Aunt Sarah knocked, and they were invited to enter.

The two brothers were sitting in comfortable armchairs.

Elias stood up. 'Good morning to you, Mistress Collins—and to you, Prudence.' She squirmed as she noticed the smugly satisfied air with which he regarded her. 'It's very good of you to bring your niece over. I've just been talking to my brother, and I may as well tell you what I have told him, namely that it is not only the children who have grown attached to the young lady.'

'Master Smith——' Prudence objected.

'Now, my dear, you mustn't be shy about admitting it, for you know it is the truth,' he interrupted her, then turned back again to her aunt. 'Mistress Collins, I may as well advise you that I hope that very soon our relationship may become—closer.'

'Oh, Master Smith! This is indeed wonderful news!' Aunt Sarah's voice was warm and encouraging. 'My husband is her guardian, of course, and you would have to consult him on any proposition you wished to make, but I am quite certain that such an offer would be well received.'

Prudence listened helplessly, clenching her fists, as this awful fate was discussed. The trap of marriage to Elias yawned threateningly before her—but not for long if she could avoid it.

'I pray you to remember I am in mourning for my dear father,' she pleaded. 'I am not in a position to consider any such proposal.'

'That will be for the elders of the Church to decide,' said Aunt Sarah.

Prudence's heart sank. That meant her fate would be decided by her uncle and Philamon Smith. It seemed useless to make any further objection. She clenched her fists and resolved to resist such a proposal with all her strength, but, looking from Aunt Sarah to Elias, she felt there was no point in voicing her objection just then. Master Philamon had a more kindly expression—perhaps she would be able to appeal to him, or to Uncle Benjamin.

It was a relief when a wail from outside the room gave her an excuse to return to the kitchen and sort out her duties. Fortunately in Martha Spinks she found a warm and friendly companion. The older woman was delighted to have the children to look after. Her own story was a sad one. Together with her beloved husband and two small children she had arrived in the colony some ten years previously. It had been one of the disaster years—they had all been struck with fever and she had been the only one to survive.

'I wished many a time that I had been taken too,' she confided to Prudence. 'You can't believe what a pleasure it is to hear the shouts and laughter of the little ones around the house. I'll see that they're all right when you're not here. Don't you worry about that.'

'Thank you, Martha.' Prudence was grateful. Martha and the children were the only consolations in her otherwise rather unhappy life.

She saw Edward most days, but never alone. She knew that he put in long hard days of work on the farm, earning his keep, and, like the household servants and the other farmworkers, he took his meals with the family. Benjamin sat at the head of the huge scrubbed table, with his wife on his right and Prudence on his left. Ironically Edward, the most nobly born of them all, was allocated a place at the very bottom.

Almost always the talk was about the new lands the settlers were about to set out to clear. Preparations were being made, food had to be collected from the communal stores, and tools made with such materials as could be found. The new settlement had been set up about seven miles to the west of the existing one, and it had already been named New Heigham.

With every day that passed Prudence felt a deepening sadness, being constantly aware that before long Edward would be leaving. Then the Collinses' house would hold no happiness for her. She almost began to think that it would be preferable to stay with the Smiths, for there she would have the children and Martha for company—but that would mean marriage to Elias, and that was as repugnant to her as ever.

The walk back after she had completed her duties in the Smith household was one of her few pleasures. The children had become more at ease with Martha, and sometimes Prudence found herself able to leave a little early in the evening, so that she could linger on her way. The days were shortening, dusk enveloping the countryside in a mantle of peace; a blue jay flitted over the path, and after watching it she leaned on the rail of the footbridge over the stream. The shallow swirling water gurgling around the stones was music to her ears. She allowed the peace to seep into her soul—until it was broken by a footfall.

Edward was walking towards her. He moved swiftly. His face broke into a smile. He quickened his pace to an eager trot and her heartbeat quickened. Had he come here specially to meet her? Involuntarily she walked towards him, stepping off the bridge, and glanced up and down the path. No one else was in sight. When she turned back he was there, right in front of her.

'Prudence,' he said, and his voice made her name into a caress.

She smiled. 'Good day to you, Edward.' They were not the words she would have chosen—they were just formalities that she felt to be necessary.

'I've been waiting to see you,' he said.

'Oh?' She had so longed to see him alone, and now that he was here she seemed to be tongue-tied.

'I just had to see you alone.'

He took her hand and led her to the side of the path, ducked under some bushes and drew her along after him. Unprotesting, she followed; the secrecy had something of the old intimacy they had experienced together when they had been escaping from the Parliamentarian forces back in England.

'What do you want?' she asked, a trifle breathlessly.

He turned her to face him, her eyes held by his for the fleetest of moments—and then he swept her into his arms and kissed her hungrily.

CHAPTER ELEVEN

A GREAT, uplifting joy pulsed through Prudence, totally irrationally, disturbingly sensual. Her blood flowed hotly and carried the longing from the sensitivity of her mouth, to create a weakening in her loins so overwhelming that her knees shook. One minute she had been alone, absorbing the beautiful earthiness of her surroundings—the next her wildest dream was being fulfilled. Edward was here. She clung helplessly to him, and his arm tightened around the narrowness of her waist, making her arch her back, bringing her body into full contact with his. Their kiss deepened, intensified, until Prudence felt as if they were melting one into the other.

There was hunger and desire in his touch, experience in his handling of her, and she could not prevent herself from responding. Surely she had been made only for him? The wonder of the sensations that coursed wildly through her gave her the feeling that she understood the whole universe, that this ecstasy was the very core of life. It was a wild embrace, an explosion of pent-up feelings, and its passion robbed her of all will-power. It was he who drew back, leaving her mouth tenderly seeking reunion with his, as she gazed at him with shining eyes.

'You ask what I want,' he murmured softly in her ear. 'Sweet wife—I want to kiss and kiss and kiss you——'

Then again his lips claimed hers, and immediately that sensual touch sent a thrill tingling down her spine. His hands caressed her and at once, with their erotic movements, awakened that wild yearning which only he could arouse in her. But now a small voice of warning was penetrating into her mind. He had called her 'sweet wife'—the meaningless title with which he had teased her in the past. If only it were true! She had told him before that she valued her purity. Now, frighteningly, a physical part of her urged her to forget— to alter—her sense of values. She longed to belong to him, totally and irrevocably—but that could never be. Reluctantly, but deliberately, she loosened her mouth from his—though heaven alone knew what it cost her.

She pushed her hands against his chest, and with a great effort forced his arms to release their hold. She stepped back, away from the temptation to bury her face against his chest. As a Cavalier, she had no doubt, lovemaking had been a part of his life, dalliance with the ladies of the court an everyday challenge. Seducing women was nothing but a pastime for him. No doubt he missed the amusement of it, now that he was here among the Puritans of New England. He had almost made her forget that she was one of them, for he held a magic charm for her. Whenever he walked into the room she was instantly conscious of his presence. It was worse when he contrived to meet her alone, for then his magnetism became an enticing enchantment and carried her away from this mundane world as surely as if he had put a spell upon her. One touch from him seemed to change her whole personality.

'What do you want, Edward?' She breathed the words again, softly, earnestly.

He heaved a deep sigh, as if she had snapped some tight-wound spring. A wounded expression took the gleam from his face. It passed in less than the time it took for her heart to contract. Every least trouble that he felt seemed to find an echo in her.

'You know that tomorrow morning we shall be leaving for New Heigham?'

She drew in a breath. 'I'd no idea it was so soon.' Her voice was a whisper; she felt devastated, unable to think properly.

He caught hold of her hands and held them tenderly. 'Come with us, Prudence.'

A part of her longed to, would have dared to say yes, but her Puritanical common sense made her answer, 'How can I?'

'You would only have to state your intention to join us. We need more people.'

He was asking her to go with *them*, not with *him*. He wanted her to become just one of the party. If he had said 'come with me' it would have been harder to resist. How could she leave, just like that?

She shook her head. 'My aunt and uncle would never consent.'

'But you are not happy with them.'

'They are my guardians.'

His mouth tightened. 'I could insist that you must accompany the party because you are my wife.'

'Edward,' she said wearily, 'you know I am not.'

'A wedding ceremony could be arranged, if that is what you want.'

Momentarily her heart leapt. He was willing to bind himself in marriage with her—it was a proposal of a sort, but empty and meaningless because it was only a means to gain the end he desired.

'Why?' she asked. 'Why do you suddenly suggest this wedding ceremony?'

'Because you wish for it, of course,' he replied in a puzzled voice. 'I know it will not make a scrap of difference to what lies between us——'

'Exactly,' she broke in tartly. It was just as she had supposed. If he had said that he understood how she felt, that he wanted her to be fully his wife, it would have been so different. 'It would make no difference. And I am sure my guardian would not consent to that either.'

'You are not under any obligation to them. You have your own goods and money.'

Was that the real reason for this insistence? Her heart plummeted. He paused and reached out for her hand, but she drew back from him. She feared her own weakness, knew her vulnerability, and dared not allow him to take her into his arms again. Her eyes were fastened to his face, taking in every flicker of expression, and she saw no sign of tenderness. He even smiled, quite coolly, as if he understood and her reaction amused him.

'Oh, don't worry. I shan't force you to accompany me.' He dropped her hands and his voice was bitter. 'We want only willing volunteers. I know that life in the new plantation will be even more primitive than it is here, but we need more people—brave people.'

He was asking her to walk away with him into the unknown wilderness. If he loved her, needed her—then she would not hesitate for a single moment. She would have followed him to the ends of the earth, but she could not bear to continue living in that sort of twilight world of marriage or non-marriage, which they had been forced to adopt over the past weeks.

He was his old arrogant, haughty self again, infuriatingly confident. The closeness that could flare into passion, binding them physically, could so quickly change into a mental wall. They were separated by it now—surely that confirmed she had been right in her decision?

'Prudence,' he said with deliberate firmness, 'as soon as I can I shall come back to claim you—and then——' He leaned towards her, fixed her with his eyes, so that it was impossible for her to retreat, and bent his head. His voice came as a beguilingly soft whisper, even though there was no one else within a mile of them. 'Then I shall make love to you so passionately that you will be unable to deny me.'

The intensity of his tone disturbed her. She had no doubt that if he really wanted he could do just that—here and now. The very idea was so disturbing that she turned from him, picked up her skirts so she should not stumble over them and dived headlong through the bushes. Her feelings were so jumbled and confused that when she stepped out on to the path again she was trembling. She did not wait for him to follow her, but hurried on towards the house. She dared not even look back. She kept telling herself that she had been right to refuse—and on no account must she change her mind.

She would have liked to slip into the house unseen, to have some minutes to collect herself, but her aunt met her on the doorstep.

'You're late,' snapped Aunt Sarah. 'And your bonnet's slipped——'

Prudence hastily straightened it. 'I'm sorry—I've been playing with the children.'

'You looked flushed too.' Her aunt peered at her suspiciously.

'I thought I was late—I've been hurrying.'

'Your uncle's waiting to speak to you. He's in the parlour. Come along.'

Prudence wondered wildly if someone had seen Edward kissing her as she followed Aunt Sarah to the parlour. Uncle Benjamin looked up as they entered. She was relieved to see that his narrow face with its little grey goatee beard was beaming at her in a friendly manner. He invited her to take a seat.

'I've been hearing good reports about you, Prudence,' he said.

She sat down on the edge of the chair and waited with her hands folded demurely.

Her uncle continued, 'I've had a visit from Master Elias Smith. Perhaps you can guess why he came to see me?'

Her heart sank. She regarded her uncle with desperation in her eyes and shook her head, even though she knew only too well.

'He has formally asked for your hand in marriage.'

'Please thank him, but tell him I cannot marry him,' Prudence said. She was surprised at how cool she sounded.

The beaming smile left her uncle's face, the goatee beard seemed to jerk forward, his face reddened and his surprise caused him to splutter, 'But—but——'

'Prudence, there is no need to play at being coy,' snapped Aunt Sarah. 'It is an excellent match, and your uncle has accepted on your behalf.'

'But I do not wish——'

'Your wishes have no bearing on the matter. You are a very fortunate girl to have this offer. Master Philamon is the most respected and wealthiest man in the colony, and it is a great honour for you to receive a proposal of marriage from his brother.'

'Aunt Sarah——'

'Believe me, Prudence, we know what is best for you, and in time you will come to thank us for making the decision,' her aunt said. 'There is nothing more to be said. Your uncle will see to the wedding arrangements immediately.'

'Your aunt is right, Prudence. It is an excellent match: you will not be far from us, and it will forge a link between the two biggest estates in the colony,' agreed Uncle Benjamin.

Everything about the match delighted her aunt and uncle. It would take her off their hands, and bring about a closer relationship with the Smiths, which would add to their prestige.

'Your uncle has most generously offered to pay for a new outfit for you, Prudence, so that your wedding-day will be an occasion of which we can be proud.' Aunt Sarah spoke as if such an offer would be too magnanimous for Prudence to refuse.

'Indeed,' agreed Uncle Benjamin. 'And of course you will not go to Master Smith empty-handed. You have the goods you brought with you, and I believe you also have a sum of money. Your good father wrote me that he would bring about two hundred guineas to assist him to set up in business here. I take it you have some such sum?'

Prudence writhed. Was nothing to belong to her? She was simply being sold to Elias Smith, and, as she looked from the thin intense face of Aunt Sarah to the reddened features of Uncle Benjamin, she knew it would be no use arguing.

'I must have time to think,' she pleaded.

'There is nothing to think about. You must be guided by us, child. It is all settled. Your uncle will speak to the pastor this evening. There is to be a farewell meeting with the new settlers, to make final arrangements, and commend them into God's care. Now go and tidy yourself up before supper—you look as if you had been dragged through a hedge backwards.'

That old saying was very near the truth, Prudence thought grimly. She stood up and walked to the door. She began to wish she had agreed to go with Edward—but how could she? Especially after she had repulsed him so positively. Where was her

pride? She fetched a ewer of water, hurried to her
room, and washed and tidied herself. She went to
the kitchen for supper, but she had no appetite. Of
course, there was no chance to speak to Edward
alone—there never was.

After the meal was finished, she was about to
help the servants with the clearing up, as she usually
did, but her aunt called her away. 'There's no need
for you to do that, Prudence. You must accustom
yourself to overseeing the staff, not doing their
work for them.' She had never objected before.

There would be much worse things to get used
to if she married Elias, Prudence thought despond-
ently. She looked around for Edward—he was with
another young man and together they left the
house. Prudence hurried after him, though she had
no clear idea what she hoped might happen. There
were many people in the street; they carried lanterns
and were making their way to the church, where all
the meetings were held.

Inside the hall those who were intending to settle
had formed themselves into a group at one side,
where they were talking eagerly together. Edward
was centrally placed among them, tall and commanding—and beside him was Marjorie Sampson.
The Sampson family was there in full force and it
was evident that they were part of the new settler
group. Prudence's despair deepened. A cold fury
seized her. How right she had been to refuse to go
along with them! Marjorie said something to
Edward and he laughed—that merry carefree laugh
that could ring out even in the most difficult and
dangerous circumstances. Jealousy stabbed deep

into Prudence's heart—he was nothing but a
womaniser, she told herself. She must put him—
and his threats to make love to her—right out of
her mind.

The meeting was chaired by the pastor, who was
on the platform with Benjamin Collins and
Philamon Smith. Elias was seated near them and
made a point of bowing with the utmost formality
to Prudence, thereby attracting all the public notice
he could. He wore an expression of such smug satisfaction that she was in despair.

'Sit here with me, Prudence,' instructed Aunt
Sarah. She was one of a row of respectable matrons.
Prudence had no wish to be in their company, but
there seemed to be no alternative.

Philamon Smith opened the meeting punctually
and began by giving a brief outline of what had
been happening at the new plantation. New
Heigham was about thirty miles distant from the
original settlement where they were now. A small
number of people had 'hived off' there, as they
called it, and had worked exceedingly hard all
through the summer, making clearances, tilling the
ground and building some cabins. They were eager
to expand their little settlement and would welcome
the newcomers. They would have to share a communal house when they first arrived, but it was
expected that they would be able to build their own
homes before the winter set in, and they would get
help from those already there.

A number of questions were asked. It was four
years since there had been any uprising by the native
Indian tribes. The present settlers had been able to

work in harmony with the Indians in the area, who had been friendly, and there was no great danger. More volunteers were invited to join the brave band, but no one else stepped forward. The meeting was about to be brought to an end when Benjamin Collins stood up and raised his hand for silence.

'Before we disperse for the evening, I have an announcement to make. There is to be a marriage between my niece Mistress Prudence Collins and Master Elias Smith, the brother of our revered leader, Master Philamon Smith.'

Prudence gasped. When her aunt had said that arrangements were to be made immediately she had certainly never imagined it would be with such speed as this! Elias stood up, bowed in the direction of Benjamin and then stretched out a hand towards Prudence, as if he expected her to get up and join him.

'Stand up, Prudence,' urged Aunt Sarah. She seemed to have risen a foot higher in her chair with pride, and the other ladies hid their envy beneath false smiles of congratulation.

Prudence remained transfixed, and horrified. They were forcing her, despite her disagreement. The smile on the face of Elias as he looked at her seemed to her positively lascivious. Did no one else see it that way? Or did they just not care?

'You all know the sad circumstances that accompanied Master Smith on his journey here,' Uncle Benjamin continued. 'His children are motherless, and my niece, who was also bereaved, found consolation in caring for the Smith family during the voyage. In these circumstances Master Smith and

I both feel it is in the interests of everyone that this wedding shall take place at the earliest possible opportunity.' He turned towards the pastor. 'For that reason the pastor has agreed that the ceremony shall be held a week from today——'

'I forbid it.'

The voice came from halfway down the hall, where the intending new planters were gathered. Prudence swung round, recognising at once that it was Edward who had called out so authoritatively and clearly, arrogantly breaking into Benjamin's speech. Everybody in the hall stared at him as he stood, tall and aristocratic, with his head thrown back, defiantly gazing around the assembly, daring anyone to dispute with him.

'I repeat, I forbid this marriage.' His eyes turned from Benjamin and fixed on Prudence with such a cold, penetrating gaze that she trembled. 'The lady knows why, as well as I do.'

There was a murmuring and movement throughout the hall as his words caused everyone to crane their necks to stare at her. A burning sensation of embarrassment and shame engulfed her and she felt so confused and flustered that she flushed, as if she had some guilty secret. What was he saying? By what right was he forbidding her to marry Elias?

Master Philamon Smith was the first to recover. 'Sir,' he said, 'you will have to give good reason for this bold statement you have just made.'

'That I will do, and gladly,' said Edward, as calmly and reasonably as if he were simply discussing the weather. 'My reason for forbidding the marriage is because Mistress Prudence Collins is my wife.'

A gasp swept through the company. Had he no sensitivity? thought Prudence. Did he not know that his words damned her reputation? Anger welled up in her. How dared he? How could he bring that nonsense up again, here in front of all these people? She had no wish to be reminded of that terrible time when, after the murder of her father, circumstances had compelled her to pose as his wife. That was over and should be forgotten—surely he was not going to reveal it to all these strangers?

He knew as well as she did that their pretence of marriage had been only a matter of expediency— and, after that statement, who would believe that there had been no consummation? She knew only too well how tongues loved a scandal, especially in such a small, remote community. She would never be able to hold her head up again among these people. She sat fuming and speechless, shaking her head.

After a brief pause while his news sank in Edward continued, 'We did not go through a formal marriage ceremony as such, but we made our declaration that we considered ourselves man and wife before a respectable pastor in England.'

That was going too far—Prudence almost rose to her feet to call out a denial. But what would have been the use? The damage had been done. Nothing she could say would restore her respectability.

'Why should we believe you? If you were man and wife, why did you not live as such on the ship?'

Elias shouted. His face had reddened with fury, for he felt that he had been made to look a fool.

'I had my own reason for that,' Edward answered him firmly. 'As for the proof—I have here a document, signed by the pastor to whom I referred.'

Prudence watched in disbelief as he held up a sheet of thick paper. 'It is a burial certificate for Jacob Collins, the father of my wife. It states quite clearly that the next of kin is Mistress Prudence Hayward, wife of Edward Hayward.'

He was utterly ruthless, she thought bitterly, using her dear father's burial certificate to prove his point. How long ago that sad time seemed now! She felt herself without a friend in the world. She had no recollection of that document being written. She had been in such a state of distress and misery that she had taken little notice of the formalities required for the burial. She had left all the arrangements to Master Kent and Edward, never thinking to ask for the certificate. Of course, Master Kent had inserted what he believed to be her married name. Anyone learning how they had deceived the good man into thinking they were man and wife would be repulsed—she would never be able to make them understand how they had been in fear of their lives. Did that document really carry the authority that Edward obviously ascribed to it? Had he deliberately set out to trap her with that document? Impossible to believe that, when it had happened all those weeks ago. There was no doubt, however, that he had taken care of it throughout their journey—and now he was producing it to ensure that she did not marry Elias.

'Bring the certificate over here and let us read it for ourselves,' instructed Benjamin.

Edward marched boldly forward. The three men all studied the paper, then looked up. 'It is exactly as he says,' the pastor announced to the rapt audience. This event added spice to what would otherwise have been a fairly routine meeting. There were a few exclamations, but mostly people were just listening in fascinated silence. Elias walked over to his brother and Philamon passed the document to him without a word. Prudence waited breathlessly for his verdict. She was sure that he would not want to marry her now—but where would that leave her?

Elias hit the paper dismissively with his fingers. 'This means nothing,' he declared. 'It's not a marriage line. I will not accept it.'

'I'm afraid you'll have to, brother,' said Philamon severely. 'I do not understand it, but I do not see how we can argue against it.'

The pastor stroked his grey beard and shook his venerable head. 'In the light of this, it would be wrong, and quite illegal, for me to perform a marriage ceremony for Mistress Collins.'

'You never told me you were married!' red-faced with frustration and rage, Elias shouted accusingly at Prudence. 'You've made a fool of me. What do you mean by it—accepting my offer of marriage?'

'No,' Prudence was stung to reply. 'I never agreed to marry you.'

Elias swung round to Benjamin. 'Did you know she was married?'

'Most certainly not. Prudence has never said a word about it to us. Nor has Master Hayward, though he has accepted my hospitality since he arrived here.' Benjamin looked towards his wife, who had been surprisingly quiet during this altercation.

'Their behaviour has been quite disgraceful.' Aunt Sarah gave Prudence a spiteful shove. 'I'm ashamed of you, to think that you've been carrying on with this—this villainous creature, even before your poor father's body was cold in his grave. Tell us!' she screamed. 'Tell us what you've been up to, you besom. Tell us what shame has kept you silent about this?'

Prudence trembled at the hatred that lifted her aunt's voice to a high pitch. She understood how awful it must for her, because Aunt Sarah had been so pleased with the match—but her wrath knew no bounds. Prudence could not utter a single syllable. She was in a state of shock and confusion.

Edward strode down the hall until he was close beside Prudence, then he rested a hand on her shoulder. She would have pulled away from it, but his grasp was too firm, his fingers seemed to bite into her bone, holding her still, and surprisingly the strength of his touch gave her courage. She sat with her eyes downcast, wondering what explanation he would make.

'My wife need say nothing,' he declared. 'The document has told you all you need to know. Tomorrow, when we set out, Prudence will go with me as my wife.'

That was all. He was taking her with him, despite her refusal. Her heart leapt—but her mind told her to be wary. She had yet to discover why he wanted her with him.

'To think that I trusted my children to the care of such a woman!' Elias, in his frustration and fury took to shouting abuse. He wagged a finger in her direction. 'You shall never even speak to them again.'

'She has made fools of us all,' Benjamin put in. 'I opened my home to her, and took in that rogue as well, because she pleaded with me to give him accommodation, and all the while they were deceiving us and no doubt laughing at us.'

'On my honour,' cried Prudence, 'whatever you may think, I have done no wrong.'

'That,' said the pastor, sternly, 'is a matter for God and your consciences.'

'Amen,' agreed Edward. 'Come, Prudence, we have to make preparations for our departure.'

He offered her his arm in a solicitous Cavalier fashion, and, trembling a little, she rested her hand in it. Without that support she would probably have been quite unable to walk. Making her way out of the hall, passing between the rows of people, who all stared quite unashamedly, among whom was not one single friendly face, was one of the most terrible ordeals she had ever endured in her life.

'You shall not enter my house ever again,' Aunt Sarah screamed, her face contorted with fury.

'We have no need to,' Edward replied. 'Except to collect those goods that belong to us.'

He was already taking charge, thought Prudence, claiming her personal belongings as 'theirs'.

'I'll throw your things outside, such as they are, and you can pick them up.' Prudence dared not look back. She was too distressed to argue.

She heard Benjamin comforting his wife. 'Hush, my dear. It would be better if—er—Mistress Hayward should be allowed to collect her own things.'

'Hmmph!'

'On this occasion,' Benjamin said firmly, 'it shall be as I say.'

'Very well, if you insist, Benjamin,' Aunt Sarah agreed. Then added spitefully, 'I certainly have no wish to keep any of her rubbish in my house.'

It was under her strict surveillance that Prudence was permitted to gather her things together and hand them to Edward to carry away. Her aunt's disparaging remarks were all the more hurtful as she realised how pitifully few items there were— bedding, pots and pans, clothing, toiletries, and the few jars of preserved food that remained. She had packed them into the wagon weeks ago in Norwich, carried them with care to Harwich, and across the Atlantic in the *Angelica*. Now they were all she had with which to start her new life—a life that would take her further into the unknown—a life in which she was still unclear as to whether she was married or not.

Edward had declared himself to be her husband, and he appeared to believe there was no need of any further ceremony. Now she had no alternative but to go along with him—but she felt if anything even more helpless than before. The relief she felt at having escaped marriage with Elias was over-shadowed by the uncertainty of her future.

She hugged to herself the secret store of gold which she carried, as always in the drawstring bag, hanging from her waist.

CHAPTER TWELVE

EDWARD piled the items on a hand-cart, while Prudence watched with a feeling of helplessness and distress. The eagle eye of Aunt Sarah poked suspiciously at every piece of bedding, and she looked into every pot, box or jar that was carried out of the house as if she suspected her niece would steal if given half a chance. A group of curious folk gathered around to watch, though they kept a little distance away for fear of catching the sharp end of Aunt Sarah's tongue. They muttered comments loud enough to be heard and one comedian among them sometimes made derisory remarks, which raised a laugh and added to Prudence's anguish.

It was a relief when Edward lifted the last box on to the cart and spread the tilt over the top. His face had been expressionless, as if set in a mould. 'Ready?' he asked.

'Yes!'

Aunt Sarah swung round and marched into her house, brushing her hands one against the other, as if they had been soiled and needed cleaning. The crowd parted to make way for them.

Suddenly from among them Elias Smith stepped forward. He leaned towards Edward, his face contorted with hatred and rage. 'I'll kill you for this,' he snarled.

Edward stared him defiantly in the eye, raking him with a derisory glance. 'Get out of my way,' he commanded. He did not falter for a single step.

Elias had to jump back to avoid the wheels of the cart. He shook his clenched fist at Edward, and the murder in his expression emphasised his words. 'I mean it,' he spat viciously. 'You'll regret you ever crossed my path, Hayward.'

Prudence breathed a sigh of relief when he turned and darted away. In a moment he had vanished into the darkness with the rest of the onlookers, but the fear she felt lingered on. She knew Elias well enough to believe he was capable of carrying out his threat quite cold-bloodedly.

Edward was a little ahead of her and she ran to catch up, scared to be left alone. She marvelled that he could behave with such calm and ease. He was pushing the hand-cart along the street as if he had not a care in the world. It occurred to her, with a touch of amusement, that he had probably never done such a thing in his life before. She fell into step beside him.

'Where are we going now?' she asked.

'I've found some lodgings,' he replied.

She digested the implications of that. 'Edward,' she asked, 'do you really believe that I am your wife?'

'Does my opinion matter?' he countered.

'I don't know. I just don't understand. I mean, how can we be married when we have never been through a marriage ceremony?'

'The pastor accepted that such a formal ceremony is not necessary,' he reminded her. 'A declaration between two people that they consider themselves to be man and wife is sufficient to make a common-law marriage.'

'I have never made such a declaration,' she objected.

'Maybe not, but to the best of my recollection you have never denied our relationship either—at least not in public.'

'That really hasn't been my fault,' she objected sharply.

'I agree, our "marriage" hasn't been entirely regular; however, I am quite happy to accept the situation as it is.'

'But I am not,' she stormed.

He stood still and set down the cart. 'Of course, if you would prefer to remain here and enter into this union with Elias Smith, I am prepared to take you to his house——'

'You know that's impossible now. He would never accept me.'

'Oh, I don't know. Maybe not in quite the same capacity—but it seemed to me he was hot for you——'

'How dare you?' she flared furiously, tears pricking behind her eyes. Had she not suffered enough, without his adding insults to everything else?

'You can't deny it.' Was there contempt in his tone?

'I have never encouraged him.'

'Ah, but then I know that sometimes you can be so innocently unaware of what you are doing. I de-

spair of you, Prudence—take my word for it, Elias
is not the right man for you.'

'I did not want him——'

'Exactly! So, you see, it was impossible for me
to go away and leave you to enter marriage with
that obnoxious bigot.'

'I refused him. I would never have married him.'

'They'd have set the seal on it next week, you
know that.'

She swallowed hard. She would not admit it, but
she had an uncomfortable feeing that it was true—
her protestations would have counted for nothing.
If she had continued to refuse there was little doubt
Aunt Sarah would have turned her out of the house,
and, with nowhere to live, no support, how could
she have survived?

He waited with every appearance of being thoroughly reasonable, aloofly patient, while she remained in mental and emotional turmoil. She felt
degraded by what had happened and that made her
angry. She was also deeply concerned about her
future role with Edward. But if he thought she
would act the quiet, complaisant wife he was absolutely mistaken.

'Well, Prudence, which is it to be?' he asked her.
'Will you make your peace with Elias and share his
bed for the rest of your life? Or come with me?'

'I have no wish to do either,' she declared tartly.
'But it seems I have no choice.'

'You have a choice, Prudence.' He paused and
his voice became harsher, with an undertone of
anger. 'Do not think I am forcing you to come with
me. I remain convinced that Elias is not the man

for you, and I make no apology for preventing your union to him, but there are many other unattached men in the town——'

'How dare you? I am not some baggage to be handed from one man to another,' she said.

'I was not actually suggesting that. Simply that you would easily find a husband. Women are in such short supply here——'

'So that's why you insist on taking me with you! Well, at least I now know exactly where I stand with you. Let us get on our way.'

He still made no move. His face was very serious. 'Think carefully, Prudence. I must warn you that life with me will not be a bed of roses. The colony we are to join is not yet properly set up. I don't know what lies ahead, but surely there will be hardship—danger—privations. I am a demanding man, perhaps sometimes a hard man. Long hours of manual work lie ahead. I believe I shall win through in the end, and it will be easier with your help.'

Exactly! Just what she had suspected! He needed her for those things that she could offer him—the goods on the hand-cart, the gold in her bag, and the extra pair of hands to work the land and make a home. He needed her. That was obvious, otherwise he would not have made that disturbance at the meeting-house. As for the hardships, she would just hope that she could cope with them as and when they came.

'I'll accompany you and help you all I can—but I still do not believe I am your wife.'

'I know differently, but I accept your scruples. Marriage and child-bearing can be a dangerous business for a woman, and especially so out here. You have my word that I shall not force myself upon you.'

His words made her sound weak and foolish— that had not been exactly what she had meant, but she was content to allow him to think so. It told her where she stood, but, remembering the passion of his kisses and his own admission that he was a demanding man, she did not entirely trust him. She sighed and wished they had been properly married—but it seemed she might just as well wish for the moon.

'Come, Prudence.' He picked up the handles of the cart and pushed it off along the street again.

'Where are we going?' she asked.

'We'll lodge overnight with the family who loaned me this cart. They're not well-to-do people, but they're kindly. You'll be safe there.' His lip curled as he said that. 'The house is so crowded, you won't be alone with me for an instant.'

They walked the entire length of the street and came to an area of salt-marshes, beyond which white sands bordered an estuary stretching towards the horizon. The land was too low to give a view of the open sea. The temperature was dropping sharply by the time they arrived at the cabin, inside which the log fire provided a warm, smoky atmosphere. It was occupied not only by the householder and his wife, who were strangers to Prudence, but by the entire Sampson family. Marjorie rose to her feet with a slowly sensuous movement, and stretched, cat-like, as Prudence and Edward entered.

'You fetched her, then,' she said to Edward.

'Yes. This is Prudence,' he said to the householder.

He did not introduce her as his wife, but no doubt they already knew that.

'Come over here, sit you down by the fire and get a-warm,' Marjorie invited, indicating the stool on which she had been seated.

Prudence hesitated. 'I'm not really cold,' she said.

Marjorie shrugged. 'Please yourself.' She sat down again, and, as she did so, glanced at Edward, raising her eyebrows questioningly. The link between them was still there. Prudence felt very much an outsider and, as a general hubbub of conversation again rose, she found a corner of a bench beside some of the children and sat quietly listening. There was a general air of mixed apprehension and excitement—tomorrow they would all be setting out on the long walk to the plantation which had been started by a group of a dozen families in the spring.

They prepared to bed down early, mattresses were spread on the floor, feather-filled cushions laid on benches. The women and younger children shared one room and the men and boys the other. Everyone seemed to take such conditions for granted, but Prudence found it difficult to sleep in such a crowded room. She was already awake when Edward called into the room, just before daybreak, that they should get up.

Early in the morning the little company set out. They had two wagons, pulled by oxen, covered with tilts. Prudence's possessions, together with the few things Edward had acquired, were loaded into the first of these, which they were sharing with the Sampsons and another family. Only the smallest children rode; all adults were expected to walk. Last farewells were said, kisses exchanged, good wishes abounded. Despite the early hour, many of the older settlers had gathered to wave off the newcomers and wish them well. There would be ongoing traffic between the two townships as trade developed, and that would increase as the plantation grew.

'Let's go,' called Edward.

He was at the head of the first pair of oxen, in the front of the convoy; he had placed his horse-pistol close to hand on the wagon. With an encouraging shout he urged the cattle forward, and as they leaned into their yokes the wagons began to roll. Somehow it seemed perfectly natural for him to be in the lead. Prudence fell in towards the back of the group, for they were all still strangers to her and she did not yet feel as if she belonged.

The track was wide and clear for the first half-mile as it left the settlement. Then they entered a shelter-belt of tall old trees and were then quite out of sight of the village. Prudence delighted to see blue jays flitting overhead in the branches, and heard the gravelly voice of a grackle and the unmistakable call of the mocking-bird. She was enjoying the beauty of nature that was all around her—then an alien movement in the trees caught her eye.

A man was there. He was watching in a furtive and sinister manner. It was Elias! She recognised him almost immediately and a chill struck through her. She remembered his threat of the previous evening—'I'll kill you for this'—and shivered involuntarily.

Edward, glancing back at that moment, noticed the stricken expression on her face. He felt a twinge of conscience—had he been right to compel her to accompany him out into the back of beyond? Would life be too hard for her? He hardened his heart. He could not have left her behind—not after Benjamin Collins had announced what they were planning for her. The very thought of Elias touching her made his blood curdle. Her protests would have carried no weight. She would have had to consent, otherwise she would have had no home; she would have starved, or fallen into a life of unspeakable degradation. She was too good, too lovely for that!

They reached New Heigham three days later. It was early evening, and they were all weary as they trudged the last few miles, wondering what they would find in this their future home. The settlement, so recently carved out of the wilderness, consisted of nothing but half a dozen cabins, scattered like wooden beads around a patch of cleared common land. When they had laid it out they had obviously been thinking of their old villages back home, and in New England, just as in old, they used the communal green for keeping their goats and chickens. It was a homely touch that pleased Prudence.

News of their arrival had reached the plantation in advance and a group of elders were waiting to greet them. After shaking hands with Edward and the other men they suggested the wagons should be taken over to a large building, prominently placed at the top end of the green.

'It's our meeting-house,' explained one. 'Our church, but we also use it for communal purposes. We've built a sort of lodging-house beside it where newcomers may stay until you have cleared a patch of land and built houses for yourselves.'

It was encouraging that several people came and helped, for there was a great deal to do. The oxen were unyoked and hobbled on the common to rest and graze. Food had to be prepared, and bedding taken into the lodging-house, and the tired children comforted and cared for. They had eaten well while on the trail, for Edward was a superb marksman. With his horse-pistol he had kept them well supplied with wild turkey and other fowl from the forests through which they had passed. His skill had earned him the unchallenged position as leader of the group.

When the immediate hustle had subsided and they had eaten a good wholesome meal, and cleared up, Prudence wandered away just to be on her own. She leaned back against the wheel of the wagon and stared across the common in the pale moonlight. A few moments later Edward joined her there.

'Well?' he said. 'What do you think of it?'

'It seems a pleasant place,' she said. 'And assuredly I shall be glad to be still. I feel as if I have been travelling forever.'

'Now that's over for a time. But I wonder—shall we live out the rest of our lives here?'

Prudence thought that over. 'I've certainly no wish to go further at the moment—but I don't know about committing myself for the rest of my days.'

'I've been told the land is good and productive,' he said.

She caught a note of excitement in his voice and recalled his dream of success. He was an ambitious man, used to luxuries, and prepared to work hard to achieve what he desired.

'Will you buy land?' she asked.

'It is not just I—but we,' he corrected. He leaned over and gently kissed her on the lips.

It was a brief, friendly kiss rather than a passionate one, but even so the very touch of his lips set her pulse racing. There was no fear of his sweeping her into his arms for there were other people moving about around the wagons, collecting things, and settling into the lodging-house.

'I'll look around tomorrow, and I'll stake out a claim for as big an acreage as we can afford,' he said. 'Then I'll start straight away to build a cabin. I want my own home—I've had more than enough of this communal living.'

She drew a little away from him. She had no love of communal living either, but there was safety in numbers, and the presence of the other people saved her having to make decisions and choices which she did not wish to face up to. She pondered his proposal to buy land—he appeared to have some money of his own, but was it enough? Did he know of the gold she carried? Was he relying on that? If he was truly her husband, then legally anything she had belonged to him. If the so-called marriage was ever consummated, then undoubtedly that would be the case. But she was still not certain that she wished to commit her life to a man she did not trust, a man she was sure had no love for her, a Royalist, a Cavalier—though now that they were in the New World that seemed scarcely to matter any more.

'I'm too tired to think straight,' she murmured with a note of apology.

He kissed her again, for rather longer this time. She felt desire in the tender movement of his mouth, as if he was tasting something sweet prior to a feast. The fire was still there between them. He had cajoled her into accompanying him quietly with his promise of not forcing himself upon her. But she also remembered those other words he had spoken as they had parted at the bridge: 'Then I shall make love to you so passionately that you will be unable to deny me.' Would she be able to hold out against him if he carried out his threat? The words he had said came back to her so vividly that she almost believed he had repeated them.

She trembled, then slipped away from him and ran towards the safety of the lodging-house. His soft laugh followed her. She was sure he knew the power he wielded over her, but she was not yet ready to relinquish her independence.

She hurried into the building, and tiptoed quietly towards the side of the big room where the women's quarters were. She had already spread out her bed-roll, and now had only to step out of her dress, fold it beside her place and lie down. For a long while she only pretended to sleep, until sheer weariness overcame her jumbled thoughts and emotions.

'I've looked at some land,' Edward announced a few days later.

She had been washing clothes in a little brook, and was hanging the clean garments over some bushes to dry. Her sleeves were rolled up past her elbows, revealing damply pink arms.

'Is it good land—not too far away?' she asked.

'Come with me, and I'll show you.' He grasped her hand. 'This way.'

His eagerness was infectious, and she followed, moving almost as quickly as he did. They dodged through the shelter-belt of trees around the embryo township, and came out into some land previously cleared by the Indians, but now deserted. He strode on up a steep and stony slope and she scrambled after him until they emerged on a rounded hilltop.

'There!' he exclaimed, standing tall and spreading his arms wide, as if he were already master of all he surveyed.

It was breathtakingly beautiful. Mixed woodland, brilliant with every hue of rich autumn red, yellow and green. She stood spellbound, breathing in the pure air, turning this way and that, and whichever way she looked she found enchantment.

'It's beautiful!' she breathed, and turned round again, taking her time to view it all. Then, remembering that this was a business transaction they were considering, she concentrated her mind. 'Is it good farmland?'

'Rich and fertile. I've been assured of it,' he said.

She scraped experimentally with her shoe at the stony soil on the hilltop. 'It looks arid.'

'Of course it is, up here.' He was evidently disappointed that she could find any fault with it.

'If we're going to invest all our money we have to be sure we buy the best possible place,' she said, and considered she was simply being reasonable.

'Agreed,' he replied. His tone suggested that his patience was being sorely tried. 'We'll go down into the valley presently and then you can run the good soil through your fingers, crumble it, smell it; you'll have no fault to find then, I'll wager. I brought you here to see where I propose to build our cabin.'

He grasped her shoulders and turned her so that she was looking down the south side of the hill. 'There. Down there, in the valley, south-facing, beside that little stream.'

He was standing so close behind her that his body touched hers as he leaned over, pointing. It was a place that could fill her with delight, but she would not—dared not allow it.

'Well?' he asked. 'What do you think, Prudence?'

'How much will it cost?' Her question was purely defensive. She was not really thinking in terms of money at that moment.

He dropped his hands from her shoulders and stood back. 'It depends on how many acres we buy.'

'How many do you think we can buy?' she asked, swinging round to face him.

'It depends——' His voice was deliberate and level. 'It depends upon how much money we have.

When you tell me, my dear Prudence, I shall know exactly how many acres we can afford.'

The gold in the bag at her waist was her own. It could buy her a return passage to England if she wanted to go back. Even here in New England, where so many things had to be made or grown for themselves, money could buy useful things, goods, household items, materials. Suddenly a basic truth dawned on her with shattering simplicity. She wanted none of those things. The only thing she really wanted was to stay with Edward, to be wherever he was, to build up a life here with him, if that was what he wanted. Above all she wanted to be loved by him. Without that, she realised with a sinking heart, she would have no wish to live at all.

If only she knew how he felt about her! She studied his face, and their eyes met because he was watching her. His expression seemed remote. He was, she was forced to acknowledge, simply waiting to hear how much money she had. It was useless to wish that she could read his true feelings—she could only follow her own.

'Turn your back,' she commanded.

He obeyed. Quickly she lifted her skirt and petticoats and unhooked the little bag of gold coins from her waistband. It was considerably lighter than when she had set out with her father from Norwich.

'Now you may look,' she said, loosening the drawstring.

He peered eagerly inside, tipped some coins into his palm, then replaced them. 'Wonderful!' he ex-

claimed. His face beamed—there was no mistaking
his pleasure. He did not hand the bag back to her.

'Is it enough?' she asked.

'More than I dared to hope. Enough to stake my
claim, and set up with a few head of cattle—I'm
going to see about it immediately.'

Disappointment stabbed into her heart. The
money had brought him so much joy, and that confirmed her worst fears. She was now quite certain
that the reason he had been so determined to claim
her as his wife was because he had known about
the gold.

He had already taken the first steps down the
hill, then stopped and glanced back. 'Come on,'
he called impatiently.

She lifted her skirts slightly and followed him.
He stretched out a hand to help her, to hurry her
along, eager to get the business attended to with
the least possible delay.

The ruling elder, who had the authority to deal
with the allocation of land, lived in a fine house of
two storeys, which had five rooms, and was one of
the largest in the new colony. Edward stated his
business and they were ushered into the parlour.
Prudence was not invited to take any part in the
matter; she sat back while Edward talked the matter
over with the elder, a highly respected gentleman
of considerable substance and piety, who was also
the magistrate. When they had come to a fair and
just arrangement Edward produced the little drawstring bag, and the gold coins were tipped out on
to the table. The required number were counted

with precision, and the remainder returned to the bag, which Edward attached to his belt.

A document was written out, stating the boundaries of the land allocated, other elders were called in and the deed was duly signed and witnessed. From that moment the land belonged to Edward. Once again he had become a man of property, although not on the same magnificent scale as at Tillington Manor, and without his title. Prudence now had nothing in her own right; she had forfeited her last vestige of independence. There was now absolutely no turning back. Her gift had made Edward one of the biggest landowners in New Heigham, but she had no status, other than as his wife—and in her opinion she was not really even that!

Life would not be a bed of roses, he had told her, and how true that was! Edward threw himself into the hard physical work of clearing the ground where he proposed to build their cabin. Prudence went with him each morning, and worked as hard as her strength would allow. She marvelled at the way in which Edward could swing an axe, bring down the highest trees, roll the trunks aside, and select those he would use in the construction.

All the men from the settlement worked together felling trees, preparing the timber and building the cabins required by the newcomers. Couples with children were given priority. One after the other the little houses were built, each to roughly the same design, which made them quick to erect.

The Sampson family, being one of the largest, had their home built first, and both Edward and Prudence helped with it. After they were housed, all the Sampsons helped in the construction of the other cabins, and Prudence could not help noticing how often Marjorie worked alongside Edward.

At last the day came when their own cabin was completed, exactly on the site that Edward had decided. They stayed on especially late that day, working for quite a while after the rest of the group had returned to their own homes. It was only the bare bones of a house, four walls and a roof. It had an earth floor, on which Prudence planned to strew rushes, but that would have to be another day, when she could find the time. Now they had done all that they could for one day, and they stood side by side and surveyed their new home.

Edward put an arm around her shoulders. 'I'd like to move in tomorrow, if you're agreeable,' he said.

She nodded, forcing herself to stay calm, as if it were a matter of little concern to her, though her heartbeat had quickened. So much could be read into his simple statement. It would be the very first time they had been alone together since those days when they had been on the run in England. In some ways she had come to know him so very, very well during that period. She knew his physical strength, his clear judgement, his courage, his taste in food, his ambition—those were all obvious. When it came to understanding him properly she acknowledged that she knew little more about him now than she had done then.

Living in the communal lodging-house had imposed restrictions on them, compelled them to be quietly polite to each other, and that had become the tenor of their days together. Each of them had set up barriers which they would not cross, but when they moved into the cabin, just the two of them together—what then? She hardly dared to think of it.

He was waiting for her answer. 'Yes,' she said evenly. 'We'll move in tomorrow.' Then, as he made no move, 'Shall we go back to the lodging-house now?'

'There's one more thing I'd like to do here first,' he said. 'You go ahead.'

She was disappointed. They did not always walk back together, and it was not the first time he had stayed behind. He never told her why, and she would not ask him. She tried to banish the thought of Marjorie Sampson from her mind, but it was difficult. Since those days on the ship Prudence had been unable to banish a belief that the red-headed girl was closely linked with Edward.

'As you wish,' she said, trying to sound casual. 'I must get back to see about making the evening meal.'

She set off straight away at a smart pace. The nights were drawing in, dusk came early, but the track was by now familiar and well worn. Only where it wound through a piece of very old woodland before reaching the settlement did she experience any unease. Sometimes there the shadows played tricks. She checked her step. Was that a man standing beside the track, pressed close to the trunk of a huge old tree?

Her heart thumped in terror. She gave herself a mental shake. What foolishness! Even if it was, she had no cause to fear him. She knew all the men in New Heigham and would count most of them as friends. They had all worked together on building the new cabin for her. As for Indians, everyone assured her that none had been seen in the vicinity for over two years. She would laugh at her own fears when she reached the spot where she had seen the shadowy figure. She strode forward, keeping her eyes fixed firmly on that dark shape—and there was something furtive about it. Suddenly it moved!

She stifled a scream—it was a man, but she could not recognise him. He drew back, obviously not wanting to be seen, and she heard the sound of his footsteps crashing through the forest. The incident had unnerved her and she picked up her skirts and ran. She had almost reached the settlement when she saw Marjorie walking slowly towards her, and glancing now and again into the trees as if she was looking for someone.

'Prudence!' Marjorie called out and hurried towards her. 'I'm so pleased to see you. I'm sure I saw Elias Smith just now——'

Prudence gasped. She was momentarily tongue-tied as recognition dawned. The shape, the furtiveness—she had no doubt that Marjorie was right. 'Yes,' she said, emphatically. 'That's who it was.'

'I wanted to ask him——'

Prudence had no time to listen to what Marjorie wanted. 'Edward's still at the cabin!' she exclaimed in horror. 'Elias will kill him.'

CHAPTER THIRTEEN

PRUDENCE spun around and ran—faster than she had ever moved in her life. She sprinted back along the path, yet wished her legs would carry her ten times as fast, for terror tore at her heart.

'Oh, my God!' she heard Marjorie gasp in a voice that precisely echoed her own fear. 'I'll come with you.'

Prudence did not waste her breath to answer. She was scarcely aware of Marjorie, even though the other girl was following so close at her heels that she could hear her heavy boots thudding on the dry ground. This was no time for jealousy or ill-feeling—Edward's life was at stake.

'I'll kill you for this.' Elias's threat kept screaming through Prudence's brain. Her mind was so totally concentrated on Edward that she could almost see him, alone in the cabin, or somewhere near by. He would have no inkling that he was in any danger. Why, oh, why had he stayed behind? Yet, if he had been with her, Elias might have fired a fatal shot!

She had absolutely no doubt that that was his intention. The furtive manner in which he had been hiding behind the tree left her in no doubt that he had come to carry out his villainous threat. He was callous enough to do it, and the opportunity was there. She was panting with the effort; her chest

233

began to ache, but she did not slow her pace for one second. She had to get to the cabin ahead of Elias. He had a good start, but he would have been moving stealthily. If he killed Edward he might as well kill her too, for she would have no will to live. She was exasperated by the petticoats and voluminous skirts that hampered her, and lifted them high.

Would she be in time to shout a warning? She imagined Edward quietly finishing off some small task, relaxed and completely off guard. Elias would have all the advantage. She knew him to be so selfish and self-centred that he could be utterly ruthless—and doubtless he would be able to find some warped justification for his actions. It was even possible that he had discovered Edward's true identity, as an officer in the King's army, wanted by the Parliamentary forces. Many staunch Puritans, even in New England, would condemn Edward as a malignant.

She was getting close to the cabin. She tried to shout, to call out his name, but she was so breathless from running that only a thin choking sound emerged from her parched mouth. 'Edward. Oh, Edward.' Her words were barely audible.

Then Marjorie shouted—yelled the warning in a strong, piercing voice. 'Hey, Ned! Have a care! Have a care for attack.'

Another time Prudence might have objected to the familiarity, but just then she had only heartfelt gratitude that the other girl was there. In that moment they were allies, both trying to save the life of the man they loved. Her chest seemed likely to burst, a stitch in her side was almost crippling, but she ignored the pain. She had almost reached the cabin—Elias was creeping towards it. He must have heard Marjorie call out. He was standing in much the same attitude as when she had seen him before, close to the bole of a tree—he held a horse-pistol, and it was pointed at the closed door of the cabin. When Edward came out he would make a helpless target.

She stifled the scream that rose to her mouth, knowing that if he heard her he would rush out immediately. Without stopping to think of her own safety she rushed on, across the open piece of land where they planned to make a garden. She flung herself towards the door, and her only thought was to prevent Edward from opening it.

'Stay inside,' she shouted.

'Move away from there, Prudence,' Elias growled.

She spun round and faced him. The horse-pistol was levelled at her head. She remained rooted to the spot. 'He's not here,' she shouted back. 'He went back to the settlement early.'

'You lie. I've just come from there. Don't think you can protect that diabolical blackguard. I'll shoot you as well if you get in my way.'

'Put that gun down, Smith.'

It was Edward's voice. It came from the woods somewhere behind where Elias was standing. Relief flooded over her. Edward was not inside the cabin. She peered into the dusky shade. It was a moment before she could make out his figure, advancing cautiously through the trees. She gasped with horror as she realised he was unarmed—and she could only

watch in a petrified state of shock as Elias slowly
turned round. He made no attempt to lower the
horse-pistol. Her stomach was churning—Edward
should never have warned him. He was too honourable to deal with a man such as Elias Smith.
But she knew why he had done it—to draw the
danger away from her and back to himself.

Suddenly, with such speed and energy that Elias
was taken by surprise, Edward ducked and sprang.
His arms stretched forward, like a wild animal after
prey, he grasped his victim and in the same instant
thrust his shoulder into his legs, knocking him over
backwards. He landed with a resounding thump,
and the horse-pistol was flung aside as they grappled
together. Then they were turning and twisting on
the ground, trying to land punches.

As she watched Prudence felt Marjorie's arm
grasping her around the waist. She had not noticed
the other girl moving up to stand beside her.
Whether the hug was to comfort or to be comforted, she was not sure.

'What can we do?' Marjorie sounded distraught.

'I don't know——' Prudence could only shake
her head, understanding Marjorie's feeling of utter
helplessness. If they rushed into the fray, tried to
separate those writhing bodies, they might only increase Edward's vulnerability. Elias would not care
if they were hurt also.

Both men were strong. They rolled over more
than once; their heels kicked up the soft earth; dead
leaves splattered around as each tried to grind the
other down. At one time Elias was on top, and
Prudence almost screamed in horror as she saw his

hands on Edward's throat, desperately trying to throttle the life out of him. With an enormous effort Edward thrust him away, pushed him back and rolled away from beneath him. He lashed out with a tightly clenched fist, a mighty blow that sent Elias crashing over. Neither would give up. The fight went on. They punched and hit with sickening thuds, breathing heavily, glaring their hatred at each other.

Suddenly she saw Elias squirm away from Edward's hold and deliver such a punishing kick to his face, with his heavy boot, that Edward staggered. Then Elias crawled towards the horse-pistol and reached out his hand.

Edward was lying still—had he been knocked unconscious? She screamed, 'Have a care—he's got the gun!'

Elias was on his hands and knees; he grasped the pistol, and Edward suddenly threw himself up from the ground and hurtled his body over the other man's. A shot rang out. Both men seemed to jerk like puppets, then fall back. They were both lying on the ground, with Edward so close to Elias that they seemed almost to be locked in a lover-like embrace. There was no movement from either.

'Edward!' she cried out in anguish, starting forward. 'Edward—my love. Oh, my love!'

She ran to where the two men lay in the dust and fallen leaves at the edge of the wood. Her eyes were only for Edward as she knelt hesitantly beside his body. His face was upturned to the canopy of trees and the darkening sky above. She was sure he was dead. She looked about him for signs of a wound.

His face was battered, there was blood on it—but no sign of a mortal injury. She turned her eyes down to his chest, fearing to see bloody traces of a gunshot wound—and her heart raced with a rush of pure joy. He was breathing. He was alive!

'Oh, my darling! My darling!' The words were wrung in deep gratitude from her heart. 'Thank God!' She longed to fling her arms around him, but hesitated, not knowing how badly injured he was.

'Is Ned all right?' Marjorie asked anxiously.

'He's alive,' Prudence said.

'Thank God for that,' she said fervently. Then with a note of scorn and triumph she added, 'As for that there Elias Smith, it looks to me as if he's shot himself.' She turned him over. 'He's dead,' she pronounced with absolutely no regret.

Prudence tore her eyes away from Edward and looked over to Elias. Blood gushed from an ugly hole in the chest of his buff-coat. His face was ash-grey, his mouth gaping open. Her mind slipped back to that terrible day when the robbers had shot and killed her father. Marjorie leaned over and closed the dead man's staring eyes.

Prudence turned back again to Edward. A bruise was beginning to discolour his cheek, but his eyes were wide open; he blinked—he was watching her. 'Oh, my dear, dear Edward—are you badly injured?' She was scarcely able to believe that he was alive, and even yet she was convinced he must be in terrible pain. 'How do you feel?'

'Marvellous!' he exclaimed with a voice so full of vigour and strength that she rocked back. He gave a great laugh, then winced and touched his battered face tenderly. 'Just say that again, Prudence,' he murmured.

'Say what?' she questioned, although she knew. Even through the bruises, dirt, and bloodstains she read an expression on his face that set her heart on fire.

'Oh, my dear, dear Prudence,' he repeated her words, mockingly—but so tenderly—increasing the bond between them. 'Do I really have to tell you?'

She glanced at Marjorie, feeling shy now to be overheard. Marjorie gave her a merry smile and winked. It was obvious that she didn't care a jot. Surely if there had been anything between them she would not have reacted like that?

Edward pulled himself up to a sitting position, making the movement with surprising ease. Prudence was amazed and delighted, for assuredly that meant he had suffered no serious injury. He caught hold of her hands and kissed each of them separately. 'You called my your love—you cannot deny it, my darling.'

She had no wish to deny it, when he spoke to her like that, but she was still shy to repeat such words of affection.

'My sweet little Puritan wife, I know what I heard and we've a lifetime ahead during which I shall constantly remind you of it. But that must be later.'

Edward scrambled to his feet, and as she watched him her joy overflowed, for she was absolutely assured that his injuries were only superficial. What was even more wonderful—he had called her his darling!

He looked from her to Marjorie and addressed them both. 'I take it neither of you has suffered any harm?'

'Not the least in the world, Ned,' said Marjorie. 'The only one who's suffered is Elias Smith, and, seeing as how he only came here to make trouble, I reckon he got his just deserts.'

'I'm inclined to agree with you,' said Edward. 'But it is not for us to judge. We have to report the matter to the ruling elder. His brother Philamon will have to be notified too.'

'Oh, those poor, poor children!' Prudence suddenly remembered.

'I wouldn't worry too much about them,' Marjorie said sharply. 'Elias wasn't much of a father to them, from what I saw.'

'I know—and Martha Spinks is kindness itself to them, but they now have neither father nor mother.'

'I reckon they may be better off with their Uncle Philamon,' predicted Marjorie. 'But there's nothing we can do about that, an' I'd better get back double quick or my family'll be wondering where on earth I've got to.'

'Yes,' Edward agreed. 'Prudence, I suggest that you walk back with Marjorie.'

'Won't you come with us?' Prudence asked. She hated the thought of being separated from him even for a moment.

'I'll stay here. You must explain what's happened, and ask for men to come and fetch the body. I shall wait for them.'

'Yeah. We'll do that.' Marjorie was eager to be off. 'Come on, Prudence.'

'You'll come back to the lodging-house as soon as you can, won't you, Edward?' Prudence asked wistfully. She wished she could have stayed there with him, but common sense told her that would be neither helpful nor practical.

'Of course. You just hurry along and make the supper—I'm starving,' he replied.

Although it was well past sunset, the stars shone brightly and the path was clear. Marjorie chattered excitedly as they walked back through the woods, and Prudence was glad of her cheery company. The terror of the past hour was still very fresh and real, but, wondrously, it was overlaid with ecstatic relief that Edward was alive, and that somehow things had changed between them.

Prudence was so excited that she was only half listening to what Marjorie was saying, and just put in a word now and again. The other girl prattled on, going over all that had happened and emphasising all the drama she would have to tell her folks when she rejoined them.

'When I think that if I hadn't been in the woods and met you—you'd never have known it was old Elias . . . an' then there'd have been nobody to warn Edward——'

'Oh, Marjorie—it doesn't bear thinking about!'

'I know. An' I was only trying to have a word with him because I wanted to find out if the *Angelica* had returned.'

'I didn't know the *Angelica* was coming back,' said Prudence.

'Yes. They only went down south a little way, to pick up some timber or something. My Barty stayed on board, because they'd have been short-handed otherwise, an' the Master promised him good money for the extra trip. But I don't mind tellin' you I'll be that glad to see him back safe an' sound. I never did fancy marrying a sailor. Seen too many of the women back home, left for weeks and months on end while their men are at sea.'

'Barty?' Prudence questioned. Suddenly she began to pay rapt attention to Marjorie's words.

'He's my promised,' said Marjorie, with a bright, cheeky smile. 'I met him on the ship. An' that wasn't easy, except that your Ned sometimes let him 'ave a bit of off-duty time to spend wi' me. I 'spect you'll know my Barty when you see him. He's tall an' good-lookin' even though he has got lots of freckles. He's sworn he'll give up the sea an' settle here wi' me—an' I can't wait ter see him again. Oh, look! There's me father come to seek me out.'

Marjorie waved her hand, called out and ran, a barrage of words spilling out of her mouth as she tried to tell him everything that had happened and all at once. As soon as he had caught the gist of it, Master Sampson hurried them to the house of the ruling Elder, and Marjorie told it all over again. Prudence confirmed what the other girl had said and very quickly he sent his servants to fetch some of the other elders. He also ordered his horse to be harnessed to a flat-bottomed cart, and a party set out to relieve Edward from his vigil and bring in the body of Elias Smith.

Prudence hurried to the lodging-house and set about preparing the evening meal for herself and Edward, and it was all ready and piping hot when he walked in. He had already given his account of the fight and its fatal ending to the elders, and, although there would be further enquiries to be answered and arrangements to be made, that was all to be left until the following day. Prudence greeted him with a warm smile—she would have liked to fling herself into his arms, but they were not alone. The families had all been moved into their own cabins, but half a dozen single young men remained, and would live there for some time to come. In addition to that, the dramatic events of the evening brought a constant stream of visitors, curious to hear exactly what had happened.

Edward answered all their questions plainly and directly, even though he was constantly interrupted as he ate his meal and quaffed down a couple of tankards of ale. Prudence was heartened to hear the comments from their fellow settlers which showed clearly that they felt little grief over the sudden death of Elias Smith. It became more and more obvious that he had not endeared himself to many people. It was even said that, by his harsh and bullying ways, he had become a disruptive influence in the settlement and an embarrassment to his much respected brother, Philamon.

Nobody blamed Edward for his part in the episode, for it turned out that Elias had made his threat to kill on several occasions. More than one man made a special point of taking Edward's hand and shaking it warmly, and telling him how glad he was to see him unharmed. If anything, the incident, unfortunate though it was, had added to Edward's already high standing.

Prudence listened with ever-increasing pride—but as the evening progressed and the other men stayed on and settled down to steady drinking and talking she became aware that Edward's patience was beginning to wear thin. He glanced around the room with undisguised aggravation. Abruptly he stood up and walked to the door and stepped outside.

Prudence watched, then dutifully, with reluctance, began to clear the wooden platters from the table. Suddenly Edward was there beside her and his hand closed over hers.

'Come outside,' he said.

'I have to clear——'

'You can do that later. It's a beautiful night.' He was deliberately tempting her, and there was nothing she wanted more in all the world than to be alone with him.

Outside, he stood with his arm around her and for a few moments they both contemplated the brilliance of the moon shining through the branches of a tall tree. Then, as with one accord, they turned towards each other, and her heartbeat quickened.

'Are you pleased that the cabin is completed?' He whispered the question.

'Is it quite, quite ready?' she asked.

'I think it is.' His face was very close to hers.

Excitement emanated from him and entwined the two of them. He kissed her gently, and her lips responded. Those qualms she had cherished about the validity of their marriage had vanished. She had no doubts, she knew she belonged to him, only to him, and for her that would never change, and it was enough.

'Do you know why I stayed behind, early this evening, before Elias came?' he asked.

She shook her head, puzzled that he should now mention something that seemed irrelevant.

He brushed the backs of his fingers lightly, caressingly, against her cheek. 'I gathered dry grasses and flowers to make a bridal bed for you—for tomorrow.'

'Oh.' Love, like a physical spasm, squeezed her heart. It gave her a touch of coquetry that spiced the query that rose, naturally and unashamedly, to her lips. 'For tomorrow?'

A wide, beaming smile spread over his handsome face. He threw his arms around her and lifted her off her feet, swinging her around. 'No!' he cried. 'Not tomorrow. For tonight.' He set her down again and caught hold of her hands. 'Oh, my darling— what are we waiting for?'

'I must clean the platters——' Her objection was automatic.

'Nonsense. We're not going back in there. You might change your mind.'

Subdued, happy laughter bubbled from Prudence's lips. She would not change her mind. But she had no wish to face the older men and women who were there. Heaven only knew what they would say.

'Let's get away quickly,' Edward urged, tugging at her hand.

Together they ran, away from the village and through the woods, hurrying as if they expected someone would try to stop them. Then they slowed down and walked, and his arm encircled her narrow

waist, and she knew she had never been so happy
in all her life. The path to the cabin was well
trodden—she had traversed it daily, and this was
the third time that day—but never had it been with
such magic in the air.

When they came within sight of the cabin Edward
halted, and stood, very still and quiet. Intuitively
she felt a change of mood in him. 'What is it,
Edward?' she asked anxiously.

'It's such a poor little house to bring you to, my
darling,' he said and there was a touch of chagrin
in his voice. 'So different from Tillington Manor.
Will you mind very much how lowly it is?'

She reached up with both hands and pulled his
head down towards her. 'I have no care where it is
we set up our home, just as long as we are together,
my dear, dear Edward.'

Then, very deliberately, she kissed him—and evidently that expelled all his doubts, for he caught
her up in his arms and carried her the last steps
towards the cabin. He kicked the door open with
his foot, and when they were inside he kissed her
before he set her down. She could smell the herbs
and the rushes within. It was dark inside and they
had no light, and she clung to him, lifting her face
happy to accept all the kisses he rained upon her.

'Oh, Prudence, I do love you so. I've wanted you
for so long—I can hardly believe this is happening.'

His words sent a thrill down her spine. 'I love
you too, Edward,' she whispered and knew no
shyness with him.

'Why have we wasted so much time?' he demanded, and the passion of his kiss told her that

he was not prepared to wait much longer. He lifted the modest linen cap from her head and his hands twined themselves in her hair, and then played with the pins of the stomacher which covered the lacings of her gown. She loved the eagerness with which he unfastened her clothes from about her and buried his face in the yielding softness of her breasts. She loved him and responded to him as wantonly as any trollop, and sometimes assisted him until he had removed not only her dress but each of her three petticoats, and her shoes and stockings, her corset and her shift. As each garment came off he flung it aside and kissed her with ever increasing passion, until she stood before him as naked as on the day she was born.

'How beautiful you are, Prudence,' he breathed.

'You cannot see,' she teased.

'I can feel you. And I've imagined you so often.' He kissed her again and then lowered his mouth, working his lips and his tongue down the length of her slender, untouched young body. He dropped to his knees and his mouth nuzzled into her most secret recesses, his face buried in that triangle of hair, awakening such a response that she moaned, and instinctively opened her legs for him to taste the moistness.

'Lie down with me.'

He guided her down until she was lying beside him on to the bed of dry grasses and flowers and headily scented herbs. He leaned over her and murmured such enchanting words of love that she felt totally cherished. He seemed to find her so lovely and so exciting, and then again he was kissing and caressing and stroking and fondling her, unceasingly, touching every part of her, awakening sensations that stole all her senses from her. It seemed that her whole being was on fire for him.

'Stay there,' he murmured. 'Don't move an inch.'

He sprang to his feet. She lay back obediently, suffused by an immense joy. He found her pleasing—and she glowed and wanted nothing more than to continue to pleasure him. Even in the darkness of the cabin she was aware that he was taking off his own clothes—she caught glimpses of the pale skin of his powerful torso, heard his quick impatient movements. She remained very still, just as he had requested, not really sure what next he would expect of her, yearning for him, certain only that whatever he wanted, she wanted too.

The warmth and weight of his body was heavy on hers; the silkiness of his skin continued to pleasure her. She gasped, with a quick stab of pain, as he entered her, then she held him close, as sensations more delightful than any she had ever known carried her away, as if on a magic carpet to a world of which she had never even dreamed.

Later, much later it seemed, she heard his voice. 'Prudence?' He sounded less sure of himself, less in command than she had ever known him.

'Yes, my darling?' she replied sleepily.

'You're all right? I didn't hurt you?'

'No.' Then added with her usual honesty, 'I found it exceedingly pleasant.'

A deep chuckle greeted that remark. 'I think you are the most wonderful woman I have ever met.'

She was suddenly wide awake. 'Do you really? Truly?'

'I assure you I would not say it otherwise.'

'But you must have met so many beautiful and elegant ladies when you were at the King's court.'

'I did indeed.' He paused. 'But there is not one of them I would change for you, my dear, dear Prudence. It surprises me, for in many ways we are very different. But I know for sure that the feeling I have for you is far, far stronger and more enduring than anything I have felt for anyone, ever before. Why else do you think I left England and followed you over here to the New World?'

'I thought it was because you were in such danger there.'

'I was in danger, yes. But for many months my life had meant little to me. I was quite resigned to execution when I was captured in Tillington—and especially so when I thought you had denounced me.'

'Never!' she cried, so vehemently that he had to believe her.

'I know. You proved that when you risked so much to set me free. Even so, it seemed as if I would never really be able to get close to you.' He leaned over and kissed her, then nuzzled his face into her shoulder. 'Oh, my sweet, sweet wife, I've been yearning for you for so long! I believe I fell in love with you that very first day when we began our travels together, and you have opposed me so vehemently that I thought you would never give in. Now I need you so much, I swear I shall kill myself if you persist in saying you do not consider yourself to be my wife.'

She reached out a finger and closed his lips. 'Do not speak so, dear husband. I know now that I am your wife in the sight of God. I need no other ceremony.'

Look out for the two intriguing

MASQUERADE *Historical*

Romances coming next month

HEARTS OF THE VENDÉE
Truda Taylor

Hortense Claviere *had* to get home to her cousin's chateau in the Vendée. Her father's last wish, before being guillotined, was that she should take the fortune in jewels he had amassed to support the Royalist cause against the Republicans.

In doing so, Hortense fell in with Raoul Duchambray, the black sheep of Ramboulard, the estate which marched with Claviere. Unknown to her, Raoul had a special purpose in returning to Ramboulard, one not to his liking, and one which would cause anguish for himself and Hortense. His integrity in question, there seemed no way out . . .

MR RAVENSWORTH'S WARD
Petra Nash

Having brought up her daughter in the country, Lady Waverton knew that if Theodora was to have the chance of a good marriage, she must have a Season. The unexpected intrusion of Edmund, Lord Langdale, and his guardian, Mr Alexander Ravensworth, into their quiet lives, provided the catalyst needed.

Alexander told himself he was simply being unusually altruistic in discreetly arranging Theodora's launch, though the beautiful, lively girl, had a far greater effect on him than he was prepared to admit – until Edmund and Theodora announced their engagement . . .

Available in December

An irresistible offer for you

Here at Reader Service we would love you to become a regular reader of Masquerade. And to welcome you, we'd like you to have two books, a cuddly teddy and a MYSTERY GIFT - ABSOLUTELY FREE and without obligation.

Then, every two months you could look forward to receiving 4 more brand-new Masquerade Romances for just £1.99 each, delivered to your door, postage and packing is free. Plus our free newsletter featuring competitions, author news, special offers offering some great prizes, and lots more!

This invitation comes with no strings attached. You can cancel or suspend your subscription at any time, and still keep your free books and gifts.

Its so easy. Send no money now. Simply fill in the coupon below at once and post it to - Reader Service, FREEPOST, PO Box 236, Croydon, Surrey CR9 9EL.

NO STAMP REQUIRED

Yes! Please rush me my 2 Free Masquerade Romances and 2 Free Gifts! Please also reserve me a Reader Service Subscription. If I decide to subscribe, I can forward to receiving 4 brand new Masquerade Romances every two months for just £7.96, delivered direct to my door. Post and packing is free, and there's a Newsletter. If I choose not to subscribe I shall write to you within 10 days - I keep the books and gifts whatever I decide. I can cancel or suspend my subscription at any time. I am over 18.

Mrs/Miss/Ms/Mr _____ EP

Address _____

_____

_____ Postcode _____

Signature _____